The Copyist's Quest

COMPANION BOOK

Pablo A. Aguilar

Table of Contents

INTRODUCTION

Hey there, fellow bookworm!

Are you ready to dive into the captivating world of "The Copyist's Quest"? Well, buckle up because this companion book is here to take your reading experience to a whole new level!

As you follow Lucien's epic journey, this guide will be your trusty sidekick, helping you uncover the story's hidden gems and mind-blowing themes. Get ready to explore the vibrant characters, nail-biting events, and powerful ideas that make this novel an absolute page-turner!

Want to get to know the main characters better? We've got you covered! Dive into the lives of Lucien, Estienne, and all the other key players. Discover what makes them tick, how their relationships evolve, and how their personal journeys shape the story's core messages.

Need a quick refresher on the plot? No worries! This companion book has a handy summary that'll help you keep track of all the important events and turning points. It's like having a cheat sheet for the story's essential elements!

But that's not all! Get ready to put on your thinking cap and explore the big ideas that make "The Copyist's Quest" so special. This guide will take you on a thrilling ride through the story's central themes, encouraging you to ponder the deeper meanings behind Lucien's experiences and the historical setting that shapes his world.

Want to test your knowledge and spark some lively discussions? Our Q&A section has got your back! Challenge yourself with thought-provoking questions and uncover new perspectives on the story. Whether you're flying solo or part of a book club crew, these prompts will get your brain buzzing and your conversations flowing.

For those of you who love to geek out on the spiritual side of things, we've got a special treat! The companion book shines a spotlight on Scripture, drawing parallels to biblical verses and offering soul-stirring reflections. It's like having a personal guide to the story's deeper spiritual significance.

But wait, there's more! This guide also shows you how the book's themes connect to the real world and the issues that matter to you. By exploring how the story's insights relate to your own life and the world around you, you'll gain a whole new appreciation for the power of storytelling and its ability to inspire change.

And let's not forget the best part—the activities! Get ready to unleash your creativity and have a blast with a bunch of engaging exercises that'll help you connect with the book on a whole new level. From art projects to community events, these hands-on experiences will make your journey through "The Copyist's Quest" unforgettable.

So, whether you're a curious reader, a student looking to ace your literature class, or just someone who loves a great story, this companion book is your golden ticket to a richer, more immersive reading experience. Get ready to embark on a mind-expanding adventure that will challenge you, inspire you, and leave you with a newfound appreciation for the power of words and the resilience of the human spirit. Let's do this!

CHAPTER 1
The Unyielding Flame

Summary

This chapter takes place in the town square of Avignon the day after Ash Wednesday. A large crowd has gathered to witness the execution by burning of Benoit, a young man of the Waldensian faith. He is condemned for the crime of preaching in the marketplace and distributing copied scriptures, deemed heretical by the Church.

As the execution unfolds, Lucien inadvertently gets drawn into the crowd and bears witness to the disturbing scene. Despite being bound and gagged, Benoit maintains unwavering faith, reciting psalms as the flames consume him. His courage and conviction leave a profound impact on Lucien and others in the crowd.

Key Characters

- Lucien (light) - A young merchant who witnesses the execution
- Benoit (blessed) - A Waldensian man condemned for preaching his faith and copying scripture
- The Bishop - The religious authority figure who oversees and orders Benoit's execution
- The Older Woman - Provides context about who Benoit is to Lucien
- The Weathered Laborer - Explains that Benoit was copying and distributing forbidden religious texts

Central Themes

1. **Religious Persecution and Intolerance**
   a. The brutal execution of Benoit for his Waldensian faith and copying scriptures highlights the harsh religious persecution and intolerance of the time period.
   b. The Church's fear of any beliefs/ideologies that challenged its authority led to the oppression and violent silencing of those deemed "heretics."
   c. The passage serves as a powerful condemnation of such religious extremism and the denial of freedom of belief.
2. **Unwavering Faith and Conviction**
   a. Despite facing imminent death, Benoit maintains steadfast devotion to his religious beliefs, reciting psalms and prayers as the flames consume him.
   b. His serene acceptance of martyrdom and refusal to recant astounds the witnesses and executioners alike.
   c. Benoit's courage in the face of brutality highlights the strength of unshakable faith and the willingness to sacrifice everything for one's convictions.
3. **Power of the Written Word**
   a. Benoit is condemned in part for copying and distributing religious scriptures and texts considered forbidden by the Church.
   b. His role as a "copyist of scripture" holds great significance and danger during this era of oppression of non-approved writings.
   c. The chapter underscores the importance of the written word in preserving and sharing ideas, even under threat of extreme punishment.

Q&A

1. What crime was Benoit accused and condemned for?

Benoit was condemned for the crime of heresy—specifically for preaching his Waldensian faith in the marketplace and distributing copied religious scriptures deemed forbidden by the Church.

2. How did Benoit respond when given a final chance to recant his faith?

When offered one last chance to recant his faith and save himself, Benoit steadfastly refused, stating: "I have devoted my entire heart to serving my Lord, and He has never failed me. How can I renounce Him now? I am certain that the next time I open my eyes, I will behold His radiant and glorious face."

3. What was the reaction of the crowd as they witnessed Benoit's execution?

The crowd's reaction was mixed, with some gasping in horror at the brutality, while others were in awe of Benoit's courage and conviction. Some turned away unable to watch, while others like Lucien remained transfixed. An undercurrent of admiration could be sensed, even among the executioners.

4. What specific details are given about how the fire consumed Benoit?

Vivid details are provided, such as the flames "leaping eagerly" and "licking at the wood and pitch", the clothing "charring and disintegrating", and the "acrid smell of burning wood and flesh". Despite this, Benoit's serene expression and voice reciting psalms is contrasted against the fury of the flames.

5. What broader themes does this passage explore beyond religious persecution?

The passage explores the power of conviction and unshakable faith in holding firm to one's beliefs, even in the face of brutal consequences. It examines the conflict between fear and courage—the Church acting out of fear to crush ideologies challenging its authority. The importance of the written word and access to scripture is also highlighted.

Scripture Spotlight

1. Psalm 91:1 "He who dwells in the secret place of the Most High shall abide under the shadow of the Almighty."

This verse reflects Benoit's steadfast faith and trust in God's protection, even in the face of imminent danger and persecution.

2. Matthew 5:10 "Blessed are those who are persecuted because of righteousness, for theirs is the kingdom of heaven."

Benoit's courage and unwavering commitment to his beliefs, despite facing persecution and death, exemplify the blessedness promised to those who endure suffering for the sake of righteousness.

3. Isaiah 43:2 "When you pass through the waters, I will be with you; and through the rivers, they shall not overwhelm you; when you walk through fire you shall not be burned, and the flame shall not consume you."

This evocative verse parallels Benoit's recitation of Psalms and prayers through the consuming fire. Though his physical body perished, his voice defiantly endured the flames until the end.

Relevant Topics

1. How does religious intolerance and persecution still manifest in the modern world, and what can be done to promote greater understanding and acceptance between different faiths?

While burning at the stake is an archaic form of execution, religious intolerance, discrimination, and violence tragically still occur in many parts of the world today. This passage serves as a sobering reminder of the brutal consequences of such intolerance throughout history. Examining modern instances of religious persecution and fostering interfaith dialogue could help overcome prejudices.

2. In an era of rapidly evolving technology and online information sharing, how can we ensure freedom of expression while preventing the spread of hate speech or ideologies that incite violence?

The chapter highlights the pivotal role the written word played during this period, as religious texts and ideas persecuted as "heresy" were clandestinely copied and distributed. Today, the internet provides avenues for sharing diverse viewpoints, but also allows hate and extremism to potentially spread. Striking a balance between free expression and public safety is an ongoing challenge.

3. What contemporary social or political movements resemble the zeal and conviction displayed by Benoit in adhering to his beliefs, even at the cost of his life?

Benoit's willingness to be martyred for his faith, reciting prayers amidst the flames, was a powerful act of defiance. We could examine modern activists, protesters, or even whistleblowers who have similarly risked everything, including their lives, to take an uncompromising moral stance against injustice or corruption despite severe consequences.

Activities

1. Debate Religious Freedom

Prepare yourself to participate in a moderated debate on the following proposition: "Religious freedom should be absolute, free from any governmental limitations or oversight." You will be assigned to either argue for or against this statement. Thoroughly research historical and contemporary examples, formulate persuasive arguments, and be ready to rebut opposing viewpoints. Draw evidence from the chapter's depiction of religious persecution and intellectual suppression. Your objective is to sway your audience through logical reasoning, rhetorical skill, and a firm grasp of the complex issue.

2. Perform a Dramatized Reading

With a small group, select a compelling scene from the chapter that resonates with you. Perhaps Benoit's defiant final words, or the fearful whispers among the crowd as the pyre is lit. Craft a short, dramatized reading based on your chosen scene, assigning roles and rehearsing your parts. Embody the characters' raw emotions and motivations through expressive voice and body language. When your performance begins, transport your audience into that tense, pivotal moment.

3. Design a Martyrs' Memorial

Conceptualize a modern memorial dedicated to individuals who sacrificed their lives upholding their ideological or religious convictions throughout history. First, research diverse examples across faiths, cultures, and causes. Next, employ symbolism through your choice of structure, architectural elements, landscaping, and inscriptions to create an experiential space evoking themes like resistance, sacrifice, and enduring wisdom. Finally, compile your visual designs and a written rationale explaining your memorial's key representations. Your memorial should honor the courage of martyrs while provoking reflection on freedom of belief.

CHAPTER 2
The Inquisitive Apprentice

Summary

In this chapter, we meet Lucien, a 16-year-old boy who wakes up early to help his father bake bread for the market. As he works alongside his father, Lucien's thoughts drift to the forbidden Waldensian scriptures and the copyists who risk their lives to preserve and distribute these texts. Lucien's curiosity about the scriptures grows, and he hesitantly asks his father what it would be like to be a copyist. His father, understanding Lucien's temptation, cautions him about the dangers of defying the Church and reminds him that their priority is to ensure the family's safety and survival by focusing on their daily work of selling bread. Despite his father's warning, Lucien's yearning to learn more about the scriptures only grows stronger, and he secretly vows to find the copyists one day, no matter the cost. The chapter also reveals that Lucien's father will be away on business in Lyon for five days, leaving Lucien in charge of selling bread at the market and looking after his mother and younger sister, Elie.

Key Characters

- Lucien: A 16-year-old boy who helps his father bake bread and is curious about the forbidden Waldensian scriptures.
- Lucien's Father: A baker who cautions his son about the dangers of defying the Church.
- Elie: Lucien's 9-year-old sister.

Central Themes

1. Curiosity and the Pursuit of Knowledge

Lucien's growing interest in the forbidden Waldensian scriptures and the copyists who preserve them highlights the theme of curiosity and the pursuit of knowledge. Despite the risks and his father's warnings, Lucien is driven by a deep desire to learn more about these texts and the truths they may hold.

2. Tension Between Religious Authority and Individual Faith

The chapter explores the tension between religious authority and individual faith, as exemplified by the Waldensians' commitment to reading and sharing the Bible despite opposition from the Church. Lucien's curiosity about the scriptures puts him at odds with the religious establishment, foreshadowing the potential conflicts he may face as he pursues his quest for knowledge.

3. Family Responsibility and Survival

The importance of family responsibility and survival is emphasized in this chapter. Lucien's father reminds him that their primary focus must be on ensuring the family's safety and well-being, which means dedicating themselves to their daily work of baking and selling bread. Lucien's newfound responsibilities while his father is away underscore the significance of family duty and the challenges of balancing personal desires with practical obligations.

Q&A

1. What is the significance of the quote from Psalm 119:105 at the beginning of the chapter?

The quote, "Your word is a lamp to my feet and a light to my path," emphasizes the importance of God's word as a guiding light. It relates to

Lucien's growing curiosity about the scriptures and his desire to seek truth and knowledge, even in the face of opposition.

2. Why does Lucien's father caution him about his interest in the Waldensian scriptures and copyists?

Lucien's father cautions him because he understands the dangers of defying the Church. In their society, showing interest in or possessing forbidden texts could lead to severe consequences, such as persecution or even execution.

3. How does Lucien's curiosity about the scriptures conflict with his family responsibilities?

Lucien's curiosity about the scriptures may lead him to take risks that could jeopardize his family's safety and well-being. As his father reminds him, their primary focus must be on ensuring the family's survival by dedicating themselves to their daily work of baking and selling bread.

4. What does Lucien's vow to find the copyists one day reveal about his character?

Lucien's vow to find the copyists, no matter the cost, demonstrates his determination, courage, and strong desire for knowledge and truth. It also suggests that he is willing to take risks and potentially defy authority in his pursuit of understanding.

5. How might Lucien's father's absence for five days impact Lucien's actions and decisions regarding the scriptures?

With his father away, Lucien may feel more tempted to explore his curiosity about the scriptures and the copyists. However, he will also have to balance this desire with his increased responsibilities of looking after his family and maintaining their bread-selling business. His father's absence may test Lucien's judgment and priorities.

Scripture Spotlight

1. Proverbs 4:7 "Wisdom is the principal thing; therefore get wisdom: and with all thy getting get understanding."

This verse echoes Lucien's desire to gain knowledge and understanding, even though it may be difficult or dangerous to pursue. Just as the Bible encourages seeking wisdom above all else, Lucien feels a strong pull to uncover the truths within the forbidden scriptures.

2. Matthew 10:28 "And do not fear those who kill the body but cannot kill the soul. Rather fear him who can destroy both soul and body in hell."

Lucien's father warns him about the dangers of defying the Church, which has the power to punish and even execute those who go against its teachings. However, this verse reminds us that our ultimate allegiance should be to God, not to earthly authorities who can only harm the body but cannot hinder life eternal.

3. Luke 12:48 "But the one who did not know, and did what deserved a beating, will receive a light beating. Everyone to whom much was given, of him much will be required, and from him to whom they entrusted much, they will demand the more."

As Lucien takes on more responsibility for his family in his father's absence, this verse resonates with the idea that those who are given much, whether in terms of knowledge or duty, are also expected to handle those gifts responsibly. Lucien must carefully balance his desire for truth with his obligation to protect and provide for his loved ones.

Relevant Topics

1. How can you balance your desire to learn and explore new ideas with the expectations and rules set by the adults in your life, such as your parents, teachers, or religious leaders?

It's understandable that you want to follow your curiosity and discover new perspectives, even if they might seem a bit controversial or different from what you've been taught. The key is to approach these conversations with openness and respect. Try to have honest and thoughtful discussions with the adults in your life about your questions and ideas. Listen to their viewpoints and concerns, but don't be afraid to express your own thoughts and opinions as well. Remember that it's okay to have different beliefs, but it's important to stay safe and consider how your actions might impact those around you.

2. With so much information at your fingertips, how can you determine what sources are trustworthy and accurate, especially when researching sensitive topics like religion or politics?

In today's digital age, it's essential to be a critical thinker and fact-checker. Don't just accept everything you read or hear as truth, especially when it comes to controversial subjects. Take the time to investigate the reliability of your sources, consider multiple perspectives, and be willing to adjust your views if you come across compelling evidence that challenges your beliefs. If you're unsure about something, don't hesitate to ask questions or consult with someone you trust, such as a teacher, librarian, or parent. Remember that admitting when you don't know something or when you might be wrong is a sign of strength and growth, not weakness.

3. How can you contribute to fostering a more accepting and understanding environment in your school or friend group, even when people have very different backgrounds, beliefs, or opinions?

One of the most beautiful aspects of our world is its rich diversity – everyone has their own unique experiences, beliefs, and perspectives. To create a more inclusive and understanding community, start by practicing open-mindedness and empathy. When you encounter someone who is different from you, take the opportunity to learn about their story and their point of view. Put yourself in their shoes and try to understand where they're coming from. If you witness bullying, discrimination, or injustice, find the courage to speak up and advocate for what's right. Look for ways to get involved in clubs, events, or volunteer opportunities that celebrate diversity and promote understanding. Remember that even small acts of kindness and respect can go a long way in bringing people together and creating a more harmonious world.

Activities

1. Journaling Activity: Start a personal journal where you can explore your thoughts, questions, and ideas about faith, spirituality, and the pursuit of knowledge. Write down your reflections on Lucien's story and how it relates to your own life. Consider the following prompts:

- Have you ever felt curious about a topic that others might consider controversial or forbidden? How did you navigate that situation?
- Reflect on a time when you had to balance your personal desires with your responsibilities to your family or community. What did you learn from that experience?
- How can you pursue your own path of learning and growth while still being mindful of the potential risks and consequences?

Remember, this journal is a safe space for you to express yourself freely and honestly, without fear of judgment or reprisal.

2. Media Literacy Challenge: Organize a media literacy challenge with your friends or study group. Choose a topic related to faith, spirituality, or a controversial issue that interests you. Then, work together to find at least three different sources of information on that topic, such as news articles, social media posts, or religious texts. For each source, ask yourselves:

- Who created this content and what is their background or agenda?

- What evidence or perspectives does this source present, and how credible are they?
- How does this information compare or contrast with the other sources you found?

After analyzing each source, discuss your findings as a group and reflect on what you learned about media literacy and critical thinking. Consider creating a shareable guide or presentation to help others navigate the complex landscape of information and misinformation.

3. Interfaith Dialogue Project: Reach out to a local religious or cultural organization that represents a faith or background different from your own. With the guidance of a trusted adult, arrange a visit or virtual meeting with a leader or member of that community. Before the meeting, prepare a list of respectful questions you have about their beliefs, practices, and experiences. During the dialogue, practice active listening and open-mindedness. Consider topics such as:

- What are the core teachings or values of your faith, and how do they guide your daily life?
- How do you navigate challenges or misconceptions about your beliefs or community?
- What can people from different backgrounds learn from each other, and how can we build bridges of understanding and respect?

After the dialogue, reflect on what you learned and share your insights with your study group or classmates. Consider organizing a larger interfaith event or project that brings together people from diverse backgrounds to promote understanding and compassion in your school or community.

CHAPTER 3
Secrets of the Quill

Summary

In this riveting chapter, Lucien, a young baker's boy with an insatiable curiosity, finds himself drawn into the mysterious world of the Waldensians, a forbidden sect hunted by the Inquisition. While selling his father's pastries in the bustling marketplace, Lucien catches a glimpse of a hooded figure whispering to a young woman in a shadowed alley. Unable to resist his curiosity, Lucien eavesdrops on their conversation and learns that they are part of the Waldensians. Despite his friend Yves's warnings about the dangers of associating with the sect, Lucien follows the hooded man through the winding streets. Armed with a bag of bread, Lucien gathers the courage to knock on the door where the man disappeared. The man, recognizing Lucien as the baker's boy who loves to write, is intrigued by Lucien's desire to help and learn more about the Waldensians. He instructs Lucien to return the next day alone and keep their meeting a secret. As the chapter closes, Lucien is filled with a mix of excitement and apprehension, knowing that he is embarking on a perilous journey to uncover the "secrets of the quill."

Key Characters

- Lucien: The curious and determined baker's boy who yearns to learn more about the forbidden Waldensians.
- The Hooded Man: A mysterious figure who is revealed to be a member of the Waldensian sect.
- The Young Woman: Another Waldensian who provides support to the sect.
- Yves (yew): Lucien's friend who cautions him about the risks of getting involved with the Waldensians.

Central Themes

1. Curiosity and the Pursuit of Knowledge

Lucien's insatiable curiosity drives him to explore the mysterious world of the Waldensians, despite the risks involved. His desire to learn and understand the forbidden sect highlights the powerful pull of knowledge and the lengths some individuals will go to satisfy their intellectual curiosity.

2. Defiance of Authority and Societal Norms

Lucien's decision to follow the hooded man and express his interest in the Waldensians demonstrates his willingness to defy the authority of the Church and the societal norms that condemn the sect. This theme explores the tension between individual beliefs and desires and the constraints imposed by those in power.

3. The Allure and Danger of Secrets

The chapter emphasizes the allure of the "secrets of the quill" and the Waldensians' clandestine activities. Lucien is drawn to the mystery surrounding the sect, despite the evident dangers associated with their practices. This theme delves into the temptation of forbidden knowledge and the risks individuals are willing to take to uncover hidden truths.

Q&A

1. What catches Lucien's attention while he is selling pastries in the marketplace?

Lucien notices a hooded figure whispering to a young woman in a shadowed alley, piquing his curiosity about their clandestine conversation.

2. Why does Lucien's friend Yves warn him to stay away from the mysterious individuals?

Yves warns Lucien to stay away because he realizes that the hooded figure and the young woman are part of the Waldensians, a religious sect considered heretical and hunted by the Inquisition.

3. What does Lucien offer the mysterious man when he follows him to the nondescript doorway?

Lucien offers the man a bag of bread as a way to initiate contact and express his desire to help and learn more about the Waldensians.

4. How does the hooded man recognize Lucien, and what does he tell him to do?

The hooded man recognizes Lucien as the baker's boy who is always scribbling on parchment. He tells Lucien to return the next day alone and keep their meeting a secret.

5. At the end of the chapter, what mix of emotions does Lucien feel as he embarks on this dangerous journey?

Lucien feels a sense of triumph and trepidation, knowing that he is embarking on a perilous quest to uncover the "secrets of the quill" and learn more about the forbidden Waldensian sect.

Scripture Spotlight

1. Proverbs 3:5-6 "Trust in the Lord with all your heart, and do not lean on your own understanding. In all your ways acknowledge him, and he will make straight your paths."

This verse relates to Lucien's decision to follow his curiosity despite potential dangers, possibly suggesting that faith can guide one's path even in uncertain times.

2. Philippians 4:6-7 "Do not be anxious about anything, but in everything by prayer and supplication with thanksgiving let your requests be made known to God. And the peace of God, which surpasses all understanding, will guard your hearts and your minds in Christ Jesus."

This passage reflects the faith of the Waldensians as they navigate dangerous situations, trusting in God and their beliefs to guide them through difficult times.

3. Psalm 119:105 "Your word is a lamp to my feet and a light to my path."

This verse connects with the theme of seeking knowledge and guidance, which is central to Lucien's curiosity about the Waldensians and their teachings. It also relates to the title "Secrets of the Quill," suggesting the power of the written word to illuminate one's way.

Relevant Topics

1. Have you ever felt drawn to explore ideas or beliefs that others around you consider controversial or even dangerous?

Like Lucien, you might find yourself curious about perspectives that challenge the status quo. While it's important to think critically and explore different viewpoints, remember to consider potential consequences and stay safe. Seek guidance from trusted adults and reliable sources as you navigate complex issues.

2. In a world where information spreads rapidly online, how can you discern truth from misinformation?

Just as Lucien had to be cautious about the information he encountered, you need to be vigilant in the digital age. Develop critical thinking skills, check multiple reputable sources, and be wary of sensationalism. Remember that not everything shared online is accurate or legal.

3. How do you balance respecting authority with standing up for what you believe is right?

Lucien faces this dilemma when he decides to pursue his curiosity despite potential risks. In your life, you might encounter situations where your beliefs conflict with rules or societal norms. It's crucial to consider the ethical implications of your actions, understand the potential consequences, and find constructive ways to express your views while respecting others.

Activities

1. Create a secret code:

Imagine you're a member of a persecuted group like the Waldensians. Develop a secret code or cipher to communicate important information. Write a short message using your code, then challenge a friend to decipher it. Consider how this relates to the need for secrecy in the chapter and reflect on how coded communication is used in the modern world.

2. Research and debate historical persecution:

Choose a historical group that faced persecution, like the Waldensians. Research their beliefs and the challenges they faced. Then, organize a debate with your friends. Take different roles—the persecuted group, the authorities, and neutral observers. Argue your assigned position, considering the complexities of religious freedom, state control, and individual rights. Afterward, discuss how these issues relate to current events.

3. Write a diary entry as Lucien:

Put yourself in Lucien's shoes. Write a diary entry from his perspective after the events of this chapter. Describe his thoughts, fears, and hopes. What does he plan to do next? How does he feel about potentially joining the Waldensians? Include details from the chapter and expand on Lucien's character. Then, write a second entry imagining how Lucien might view these same events looking back as an adult. Compare the two perspectives.

CHAPTER 4
Whispers in the Market

Summary

In this chapter, Lucien returns to the bustling marketplace of Avignon, his mind preoccupied with the previous day's encounter and the promise of a clandestine meeting. As he goes about his duties at his father's bread stall, he becomes acutely aware of the changing atmosphere around him. Whispers about the Waldensians and the looming threat of the Inquisition permeate the air, turning the once-lively market into a hotbed of tension and suspicion. Lucien overhears various conversations that hint at the growing boldness of the Waldensians and the potential consequences. Throughout the day, he grows increasingly anxious, feeling as if unseen eyes are watching his every move. A cryptic warning from a customer further heightens his sense of unease. As he prepares to leave for home, doubting his desire to learn more about the Waldensians, he encounters the hooded figure again. Despite his hesitation, Lucien follows the man into the city's shadowy depths, driven by his determination to uncover the truth.

Key Characters

- Lucien - The protagonist, a young boy working at his father's bread stall
- The hooded figure - A mysterious man associated with the Waldensians
- The elderly man - A gossiping customer discussing the Waldensians
- The cautious vendor - Someone advocating for keeping quiet about Church affairs
- The cryptic customer - A man who warns Lucien to be careful

Central Themes

1. The Spread of Dangerous Information:

This theme is central to the chapter, as whispers about the Waldensians circulate through the marketplace. The once-ordinary setting becomes a hub of tension and suspicion as people discuss forbidden topics more openly, highlighting how information can transform social dynamics.

2. Growing Awareness of Risk and Consequence:

Lucien's increasing anxiety throughout the day reflects his developing understanding of the dangers associated with his curiosity. This theme explores the loss of innocence as he realizes the potential consequences of involving himself with the Waldensians.

3. The Conflict Between Curiosity and Safety:

Despite the palpable tension and warnings, Lucien still chooses to follow the hooded figure at the end of the chapter. This theme underscores the internal struggle between the desire for knowledge and the instinct for self-preservation, a central conflict in coming-of-age narratives.

Q&A

1. Where is the story set?

The story is set in the marketplace of Avignon, a city in medieval France.

2. What group is being discussed in whispers throughout the marketplace?

The Waldensians, a Christian sect considered heretical by the Catholic Church, are the subject of hushed conversations.

3. How does Lucien's perception of the marketplace change in this chapter?

Lucien begins to see the once-familiar marketplace as a tense, potentially dangerous place filled with suspicion and hidden meanings.

4. What warning does a customer give to Lucien?

A customer tells Lucien, "These are dark times. Be careful who you trust," highlighting the atmosphere of suspicion.

5. Who does Lucien encounter at the end of the chapter?

At the end of the chapter, Lucien bumps into the hooded figure he met the previous day, who then tells him to follow quickly.

Scripture Spotlight

1. James 1:19 "Know this, my beloved brothers: let every person be quick to hear, slow to speak, slow to anger."

This verse connects with Lucien's observant behavior in the marketplace. He's quick to listen to the conversations around him but cautious about speaking or reacting, which aligns with the need for discretion in the tense atmosphere described in the chapter.

2. Proverbs 10:19 "When words are many, transgression is not lacking, but whoever restrains his lips is prudent."

This verse relates to the gossiping and whispering in the marketplace, and the vendor's advice to keep quiet about Church affairs.

3. Ephesians 5:15-16 "Look carefully then how you walk, not as unwise but as wise, making the best use of the time, because the days are evil."

This verse aligns with the overall atmosphere of caution and the need for wisdom in dangerous times, which is a key theme in the chapter.

Relevant Topics

1. How do you navigate social media when controversial topics are being discussed?

Like Lucien in the marketplace, you might find yourself surrounded by whispers and rumors online. Be cautious about what you share or engage with. Remember that digital footprints can have real-world consequences.

2. Have you ever felt peer pressure to join discussions about sensitive topics?

You might relate to Lucien's curiosity and desire to be involved. It's natural to want to understand what's happening around you. However, it's important to consider the risks and decide if and how you want to participate. Don't be afraid to step back if you feel uncomfortable or unsure.

3. In a world where privacy seems increasingly scarce, how do you protect your personal information while staying connected?

Lucien feels watched in the marketplace, much like you might feel observed online. Be mindful of what you share on social media and other platforms. Use privacy settings, be cautious about accepting friend requests from strangers, and think twice before posting sensitive information. Just as Lucien had to navigate a changing social landscape, you need to be aware of the digital footprint you're creating and its potential long-term impacts.

Activities

1. Create a social media simulation:

Design a mock social media platform that reflects the tension and rumors of the marketplace in the chapter. Create profiles for different characters (like Lucien, the vendor, the hooded figure) and write posts or messages they might share. Consider how information spreads, who's watching, and the consequences of what's shared. Then, analyze how this compares to real-world social media dynamics.

2. Conduct a "Whisper Down the Lane" experiment:

Gather a group of friends. Start with a complex, multi-sentence message about a controversial topic (like the Waldensians in the chapter). Whisper it to the first person, then have each person whisper what they heard to the next. Compare the final message to the original. Discuss how information changes as it spreads and relate this to both the chapter and modern information sharing.

3. Write and perform a marketplace scene:

Based on the chapter, write a short script depicting a tense conversation in the marketplace. Include characters representing different viewpoints— perhaps a gossip, a cautious vendor, and a curious bystander like Lucien. Perform the scene with friends, focusing on conveying the underlying tension through body language and tone. Afterward, discuss how it feels to live in an atmosphere of suspicion and how this might relate to certain situations in today's world.

CHAPTER 5
The Forbidden Scriptures

Summary

In this pivotal chapter, Lucien follows the mysterious hooded man, now revealed as Gilbert, to a hidden sanctuary where he encounters the forbidden scriptures of the Waldensians. As Lucien immerses himself in these texts, he experiences a profound spiritual awakening, discovering a message of love and grace that starkly contrasts with the fear-based doctrines he's known all his life. Gilbert shares the poignant story of Benoit, a recently martyred Waldensian, recounting a powerful prayer session that showcases the deep faith of their community. Deeply moved by both the scriptures and Benoit's story, Lucien grapples with the implications of this new knowledge. Despite understanding the grave dangers involved, Lucien makes the life-altering decision to join the Waldensians, committing himself to their cause and beliefs. This chapter marks a significant turning point in Lucien's journey, as he chooses to embrace a path that will likely lead to persecution but aligns with his newfound understanding of faith and truth.

Key Characters

- Lucien - The protagonist, a young boy experiencing a spiritual awakening
- Gilbert (bright promise) - The hooded man, revealed to be a leader among the Waldensians
- Benoit - A recently executed Waldensian, whose story deeply affects Lucien
- God - Though not a physical character, the concept of God plays a central role in Lucien's transformation

Central Themes

1. Spiritual Awakening and Transformation:

This theme is central to the chapter, as Lucien experiences a profound shift in his understanding of faith. His encounter with the forbidden scriptures and Gilbert's teachings leads to a spiritual revelation, challenging his previous beliefs and setting him on a new path.

2. The Power of Forbidden Knowledge:

The chapter explores how access to suppressed information can radically change one's worldview. The Waldensian scriptures, hidden from the public by the Church, serve as a catalyst for Lucien's transformation, highlighting the potential impact of knowledge deemed dangerous by authorities.

3. Personal Sacrifice for Beliefs:

This theme is embodied in Benoit's martyrdom and Lucien's decision to join the Waldensians despite the risks. It explores the idea of standing up for one's beliefs in the face of persecution, and the personal cost that can come with embracing a controversial faith or ideology.

Q&A

1. Who is Gilbert and what role does he play in the story?

Gilbert is the hooded man who leads Lucien to the hidden sanctuary. He's a leader among the Waldensians who introduces Lucien to their forbidden scriptures and shares the story of Benoit.

2. How does the chapter describe the Waldensian sanctuary?

The sanctuary is described as a hidden room with a floor-to-ceiling bookshelf filled with leather-bound volumes and yellowed scrolls. It's dimly lit by candles and has a table and chairs.

3. What does Lucien discover in the forbidden scriptures?

Lucien discovers a message of love, grace, and a personal relationship with God, which contrasts sharply with the fear-based teachings of the Church he's known.

4. Who was Benoit and what happened to him?

Benoit was a Waldensian and Gilbert's student who was recently executed (burned at the stake) for his beliefs. His story and prayer deeply impact Lucien.

5. What decision does Lucien make at the end of the chapter?

Despite understanding the dangers, Lucien decides to join the Waldensians, committing himself to their cause and beliefs.

Scripture Spotlight

1. John 8:32 "And you will know the truth, and the truth will set you free."

This verse directly relates to Lucien's experience of discovering the Waldensian scriptures and feeling liberated by their message.

2. Matthew 5:14-16 "You are the light of the world. A city set on a hill cannot be hidden. Nor do people light a lamp and put it under a basket, but on a stand, and it gives light to all in the house. In the same way, let your light shine before others, so that they may see your good works and give glory to your Father who is in heaven."

This verse connects with the Waldensians' mission to spread their understanding of faith despite persecution, as exemplified by Benoit's story.

3. Romans 12:2 "Do not be conformed to this world, but be transformed by the renewal of your mind, that by testing you may discern what is the will of God, what is good and acceptable and perfect."

This verse reflects Lucien's transformation as he encounters new ideas and chooses to follow a different path, despite the potential negative consequences.

Relevant Topics

1. Have you ever encountered ideas that challenged your existing beliefs? How did you handle it?

Like Lucien, you might find yourself exposed to new perspectives that conflict with what you've always been taught. It's natural to feel confused or conflicted. Take time to research, reflect, and discuss these ideas with trusted individuals. Remember, it's okay to question and reevaluate your beliefs as you grow and learn.

2. In a world where cancel culture is prevalent, how do you stand up for your beliefs while respecting others?

Lucien commits to a path that could lead to severe consequences, much like how expressing certain views today can lead to social backlash. It's crucial to stand up for what you believe in, but do so with empathy and respect for others. Engage in constructive dialogues, be open to learning from different perspectives, and express your views in a way that invites conversation rather than conflict. Remember, it's possible to disagree with someone's ideas without attacking them personally.

3. Have you ever felt pressured to hide your beliefs or interests for fear of judgment or consequences?

Lucien risks everything to join the Waldensians. While your situation may not be as extreme, you might face peer pressure or societal expectations that conflict with your personal beliefs or passions. It's important to stay true to yourself, but also to consider the potential consequences of your actions and find safe ways to express yourself.

Activities

1. Create a "Forbidden Book" Journal:

Design and create your own "forbidden book" journal. Use an old hardcover book or a blank journal, and decorate it to look ancient and secretive. Inside, write down ideas, beliefs, or philosophies that you find inspiring or transformative, but that might be considered controversial or unconventional. Reflect on why these ideas resonate with you and how they challenge your existing beliefs. Keep this journal private, like the Waldensians' hidden scriptures.

2. Organize a "Sanctuary Debate":

Gather a group of friends and recreate the atmosphere of the hidden sanctuary. Choose a controversial topic relevant to teenagers today (e.g., social media use, climate change, education reform). Assign roles: some as "Gilbert" presenting new ideas, others as "Lucien" hearing them for the first time. Debate the topic from these perspectives, focusing on respectful dialogue and the courage to express and consider new viewpoints. Afterward, discuss how it felt to be in each role.

3. Write a "Modern Benoit" Story:

Research a modern-day activist or whistleblower who risked their safety or freedom to stand up for their beliefs. Write a short story or essay from their perspective, similar to Gilbert's account of Benoit. Include a powerful "prayer" or speech that encapsulates their motivations and hopes. Reflect on the similarities and differences between their situation and Benoit's, considering the risks and potential consequences of standing up for one's beliefs in today's world.

CHAPTER 6
A Dangerous Encounter

Summary

In this gripping chapter, Lucien and Gilbert navigate the hidden tunnels of
the Waldensian sanctuary, engaging in a profound discussion about the
Church's corruption and persecution of truth-seekers. Their journey takes a
perilous turn when they encounter an Inquisitor and his henchman, leading
to a tense confrontation where Lucien and Gilbert's faith is tested against
the Inquisitor's threats. The situation appears dire until a providential
thunderclap plunges the tunnels into darkness, allowing our protagonists to
make a daring escape. As they flee through the labyrinthine passages,
pursued by their enemies, Lucien's thoughts turn to the forbidden
scriptures, seeking strength and guidance in his newfound faith. This chapter
vividly illustrates the dangers faced by the Waldensians, the conflict
between established religious authority and those seeking spiritual truth,
and the power of faith in moments of extreme peril.

Key Characters

- Lucien - The protagonist, a young convert to the Waldensian faith
- Gilbert - Lucien's mentor and guide in the Waldensian movement
- The Inquisitor - A menacing figure representing the Church's
  authority and persecution
- The Inquisitor's henchman - The unseen assailant who initially grabs
  Lucien

Central Themes

1. Persecution and Religious Intolerance:

This theme is central to the chapter, as exemplified by the Inquisitor's aggressive pursuit of Lucien and Gilbert. It highlights the historical conflict between established religious authorities and those seeking alternative spiritual paths, demonstrating the dangers faced by groups like the Waldensians.

2. Faith Under Pressure:

The chapter explores how faith is tested and potentially strengthened in moments of extreme danger. Lucien and Gilbert's unwavering belief in their cause, even when faced with threats from the Inquisitor, showcases the power of conviction in the face of adversity.

3. Divine Providence:

The timely thunderclap that allows Lucien and Gilbert to escape suggests a theme of divine intervention or providence. This reinforces the idea that their faith, despite being persecuted, may have divine support, providing hope and reassurance in their dangerous quest for religious truth.

Q&A

1. What does Gilbert say about the Church's motivation for persecuting groups like the Waldensians?

Gilbert explains that the Church has become corrupted by power and fears the light of truth because it threatens to expose their hypocrisy and greed.

2. How does Lucien initially get caught by the Inquisition?

While walking through the tunnels, distracted by his thoughts, Lucien is grabbed by an unseen assailant hiding in the shadows.

3. What accusation does the Inquisitor make against Lucien and Gilbert?

The Inquisitor accuses them of being heretics who spread "poisonous lies" and sow discord among the faithful.

4. What unexpected event allows Lucien and Gilbert to escape?

A sudden, deafening crack of thunder shakes the tunnels and plunges everything into darkness, providing an opportunity for them to flee.

5. What does Lucien think about as they're escaping through the tunnels?

As they flee, Lucien's mind turns to the forbidden scriptures, longing to draw strength and guidance from their sacred pages.

Scripture Spotlight

1. Psalm 27:1 "The Lord is my light and my salvation; whom shall I fear? The Lord is the stronghold of my life; of whom shall I be afraid?"

This verse reflects Lucien and Gilbert's courage in the face of danger from the Inquisitor.

2. John 15:20 "Remember the word that I said to you: 'A servant is not greater than his master.' If they persecuted me, they will also persecute you. If they kept my word, they will also keep yours."

This verse relates to the persecution that Lucien and Gilbert face as Waldensians, drawing a parallel to the persecution of early Christians.

3. Psalm 91:1-2 "He who dwells in the shelter of the Most High will abide in the shadow of the Almighty. I will say to the Lord, 'My refuge and my fortress, my God, in whom I trust.'"

This verse connects with the theme of divine providence in the chapter, particularly the thunderclap that allows Lucien and Gilbert to escape, suggesting God's protection over them.

Providential Events in the Bible

Here are some examples from the Bible where providential events occurred, and divine intervention helped individuals out of difficult situations. Can you think of some more?

- **The Exodus** (Exodus 14): When the Israelites were trapped between the Red Sea and the Egyptian army, God parted the Red Sea through Moses' staff, allowing the Israelites to escape on dry ground and subsequently drowning the pursuing Egyptian forces.
- **Joshua Stops the Sun** (Joshua 10:12-14): During a battle against the Amorites, Joshua prayed for the sun and moon to stand still so the Israelites could complete their victory. God answered, extending the day until Israel defeated their enemies.
- **Hezekiah's Illness and Recovery** (2 Kings 20:1-11): King Hezekiah fell gravely ill, and the prophet Isaiah told him to set his house in order. Hezekiah prayed to God, who added fifteen years to his life and provided a sign by making the shadow on a sundial move backward.
- **The Fiery Furnace** (Daniel 3): Shadrach, Meshach, and Abednego refused to worship King Nebuchadnezzar's golden statue and were thrown into a blazing furnace. God protected them, and they emerged unharmed, with a divine figure appearing alongside them in the fire.
- **Peter's Escape from Prison** (Acts 12:6-11): The apostle Peter was imprisoned by King Herod. The night before his trial, an angel of the Lord appeared, freeing Peter from his chains and leading him out of the prison unnoticed by the guards.
- **Paul and Silas in Prison** (Acts 16:25-26): While imprisoned for preaching the gospel, Paul and Silas prayed and sang hymns. Suddenly, a violent earthquake shook the prison, opening the doors and loosening their chains.

Relevant Topics

1. How do you navigate conflicts between established authorities and new ideas or information?

In today's world of rapid information spread and changing social norms, you might encounter ideas that challenge established beliefs, similar to how the Waldensians challenged the Church. Approach new information critically: research from reliable sources, consider different perspectives, and don't be afraid to question established norms. However, also be aware of the potential consequences of openly challenging powerful institutions or widely held beliefs.

2. Have you ever experienced a moment where unexpected circumstances helped you out of a difficult situation?

Lucien and Gilbert's escape is aided by a sudden thunderclap, which could be seen as a stroke of luck or divine intervention. In your life, you might have experienced fortunate coincidences or unexpected help in challenging times. Reflect on these moments: how did they affect you? While it's important to rely on your own efforts and planning, staying open to unexpected opportunities or help can sometimes lead to surprising solutions in difficult situations. Does faith play a role in acknowledging these events as divine intervention?

3. In times of stress or danger, where do you find your strength and courage?

Lucien thinks of the forbidden scriptures for guidance during their escape. In your life, you might face stressful situations that require courage—like standing up to bullies or making difficult decisions. Reflect on what gives you strength: it could be your personal beliefs, supportive friends and family, inspiring role models, or your own past experiences of overcoming challenges. Having a source of inner strength can help you navigate difficult situations.

Activities

1. Create an Escape Room Challenge:

Design a mini escape room based on Lucien and Gilbert's experience. Use your room or a designated area in your house. Create puzzles and clues related to the Waldensian beliefs and the Inquisition's pursuit. Hide a "forbidden scripture" as the final prize. Invite friends to solve the puzzles within a set time limit. After the activity, discuss how it felt to be pursued and how it compares to the challenges faced by persecuted groups throughout history and in the present day.

2. Write a Dual-Perspective Journal:

Write two journal entries about the encounter with the Inquisitor. First, write from Lucien's perspective, describing his fears, hopes, and the strength he draws from his newfound faith. Then, write from the Inquisitor's point of view, exploring his motivations and beliefs. Reflect on how the same event can be perceived differently based on one's position and beliefs. Share your entries with friends or family and discuss the complexities of conflicts driven by differing ideologies.

3. Create a "Tunnel Navigation" Game:

Design a simple board game that simulates Lucien and Gilbert's escape through the tunnels. Create a maze-like board with various paths, obstacles, and decision points. Include cards or prompts that represent challenges (like encountering Inquisitors) and advantages (like the thunderclap). The goal is to escape the tunnels while avoiding capture. After playing, discuss how the game reflects real-life situations where you must make quick decisions under pressure. Consider how faith, knowledge, or preparation might influence these decisions.

CHAPTER 7
The Merchant's Guise

Summary

In this pivotal chapter, Lucien and Gilbert, having narrowly escaped the Inquisition, seek refuge in Avignon's dawn-lit streets. They find sanctuary with Bellamy, a skilled craftsman and Waldensian ally, who transforms them into convincing merchant disguises. This metamorphosis goes beyond mere appearance, as Lucien embraces a new persona that will aid in his mission to spread the Waldensian faith. Bellamy's generosity extends to providing them with a cart, goods, and most preciously, a copy of Scripture for Lucien. The chapter sets the stage for their impending journey to Grenoble, where Lucien will begin his new life as a merchant for two weeks before transitioning to scriptorium training in the mountains. As they depart, Lucien grapples with the bittersweet reality of leaving his old life behind, while simultaneously feeling eager anticipation for his newfound purpose in spreading truth in a world of darkness.

Key Characters

- Lucien - The protagonist, adapting to his new role as a Waldensian and disguised merchant
- Gilbert - Lucien's mentor and guide in the Waldensian movement
- Bellamy (fine friend) - An old Waldensian ally who provides crucial assistance and disguises
- The Inquisition - Though not physically present, their threat looms over the chapter's events

Central Themes

1. Adaptation and Transformation:

This theme is central to the chapter, as Lucien physically and mentally transforms into a merchant. It highlights the necessity of adaptability in the face of adversity and the power of assuming new identities to survive and thrive in dangerous circumstances. This transformation also symbolizes Lucien's deeper personal and spiritual growth as he embraces his new life as a Waldensian.

2. The Power of Community and Allies:

Bellamy's crucial assistance demonstrates the importance of a supportive network in times of need. This theme underscores how the Waldensian community looks after its own, providing not just physical aid but also the means to continue their mission. It illustrates the strength found in unity and shared beliefs.

3. Faith and Purpose in the Face of Danger:

Throughout the chapter, Lucien's commitment to his newfound faith remains steadfast despite the risks. The provision of the Scripture and his anticipation of spreading the Waldensian message highlight how a sense of purpose can give individuals strength to persevere through challenging circumstances. This theme explores the motivating power of belief and the willingness to sacrifice for a greater cause.

Q&A

1. Who is Bellamy and how does he help Lucien and Gilbert?

Bellamy is an old Waldensian ally who provides Lucien and Gilbert with merchant disguises, a cart, goods to sell, and a copy of the Scriptures. He also gives them a place to rest and hide from the Inquisition.

2. What is the significance of the merchant disguise for Lucien?

The merchant disguise allows Lucien to blend in and travel freely, enabling him to carry and spread the forbidden scriptures without arousing suspicion. It also represents his transformation and new role in the Waldensian movement.

3. Where are Lucien and Gilbert planning to go after leaving Avignon?

They are planning to journey to Grenoble, which is a six-day trip from Avignon.

4. What is Lucien's plan once they reach Grenoble?

Lucien will work as a merchant for about two weeks before transitioning to training in a scriptorium in the mountains.

5. What important item does Bellamy give to Lucien, and why is it significant?

Bellamy gives Lucien a copy of the Scriptures. This is significant because it's a forbidden text that Lucien can now use to study and spread the Waldensian faith, despite the great risk associated with possessing it.

Scripture Spotlight

1. Ephesians 6:10-11 "Finally, be strong in the Lord and in the strength of his might. Put on the whole armor of God, that you may be able to stand against the schemes of the devil."

This verse relates to Lucien and Gilbert's need to disguise themselves and stay strong in their faith despite persecution.

2. Matthew 10:16 "Behold, I am sending you out as sheep in the midst of wolves, so be wise as serpents and innocent as doves."

This verse connects with the theme of Lucien and Gilbert needing to be clever in their disguises while maintaining their faith and purpose.

3. Proverbs 11:14 "Where there is no guidance, a people falls, but in an abundance of counselors there is safety."

This verse reflects the importance of Bellamy's role in providing guidance and assistance to Lucien and Gilbert, highlighting the theme of community support.

Relevant Topics

1. Have you ever had to adapt to a new environment or role that felt completely different from your usual self?

Like Lucien adopting his merchant disguise, you might face situations where you need to adapt to new environments, such as starting a new school or job. This can feel challenging, but it's also an opportunity for personal growth. Consider how you can use your strengths in new ways while staying true to your core values.

2. How do you balance blending in with a group while maintaining your individual identity?

Lucien had to blend in as a merchant while holding onto his Waldensian beliefs. In your life, you might feel pressure to conform to peer groups or societal expectations. It's important to find a balance between fitting in and staying true to yourself. Reflect on which aspects of your identity are most important to you and how you can express them authentically.

3. Who are the "Bellamys" in your life—the people who support and guide you through difficult times?

Just as Bellamy provided crucial help to Lucien and Gilbert, you likely have people in your life who offer support and guidance. These might be family members, teachers, mentors, or close friends. Recognize the value of these relationships and consider how you can also be a supportive figure for others in your community.

Activities

1. Create Your Alter Ego:

Design a merchant alter ego for yourself, similar to Lucien's disguise. Choose a name, backstory, and specialty goods to sell. Draw or describe your character's appearance and create a small inventory of items. Then, write a short story or journal entry from your merchant's perspective, detailing a day in their life or a challenging situation they face. Reflect on how this exercise relates to adapting to new situations in your own life.

2. Write a Merchant's Sales Pitch:

Compose a short sales pitch for one of the items Lucien might be selling (e.g., spices, silk). Research the item's uses and value in medieval times. Practice delivering your pitch to family or friends, focusing on being persuasive while maintaining your cover.

3. Host a "Blending In" Fashion Challenge:

Gather a group of friends and challenge each other to create disguises using only items found in your homes. The goal is to transform into a character that could blend into a specific setting (e.g., a busy marketplace, a fancy restaurant, or a sports event). Present your disguises to each other and vote on the most convincing ones. Discuss the power of appearance in shaping perceptions and how this relates to identity and self-expression in your daily lives.

CHAPTER 8
Estienne's Folly

Summary

In this chapter, Lucien has settled into his role as a merchant in Grenoble, using his cover to discreetly spread the Waldensian faith. During a typical day of haggling in the bustling marketplace, the routine is shattered by the arrival of Estienne, a bold young preacher who publicly denounces the Church's corruption and advocates for direct access to the Scriptures. This reckless act of defiance attracts the attention of the Inquisition, forcing Estienne to flee. In a brief but significant exchange, Lucien and Estienne connect, hinting at a larger network of believers. As the chaos subsides, Lucien discovers a cryptic note inviting him to a secret meeting, presenting him with a dangerous but potentially crucial opportunity to deepen his involvement in the Waldensian movement. The chapter highlights the tension between public proclamation and covert dissemination of beliefs, while also expanding Lucien's world and the scope of his mission.

Key Characters

- Lucien - The protagonist, now working as a merchant while secretly spreading Waldensian beliefs
- Estienne (crown) - A bold young preacher who publicly challenges the Church
- The Farmer - A stubborn customer who haggles with Lucien, representing everyday life in the marketplace
- The Inquisitor - The Church official who orders Estienne's arrest
- The Soldiers - Those who attempt to capture Estienne

Central Themes

1. Public Proclamation vs. Covert Dissemination:

This theme is central to the chapter, contrasting Lucien's careful, secretive approach to spreading the Waldensian faith with Estienne's bold, public proclamation. It explores the tension between the desire to openly share one's beliefs and the need for caution in a hostile environment, raising questions about the most effective and safest ways to spread ideas in the face of persecution.

2. The Power and Danger of Words:

The chapter highlights how words can be both powerful and dangerous. Estienne's preaching stirs up the crowd and challenges the established order, demonstrating the potential of speech to incite change. However, it also brings swift retribution from the authorities, underlining the risks associated with speaking out against powerful institutions.

3. Expanding Networks of Resistance:

This theme is introduced through Lucien's interaction with Estienne and the mysterious note he receives. It suggests that the Waldensian movement is larger and more organized than Lucien initially realized, hinting at a complex network of believers working together. This theme explores how resistance movements grow and connect in hostile environments.

Q&A

1. What is Lucien's cover occupation in Grenoble?

Lucien is working as a merchant, selling goods in the marketplace while secretly spreading the Waldensian faith.

2. Who is Estienne and what does he do that causes a commotion?

Estienne is a young preacher who publicly denounces the Church's corruption and advocates for people to read the Scriptures themselves, causing an uproar in the marketplace.

3. How do the authorities react to Estienne's preaching?

The Inquisitor and soldiers attempt to arrest Estienne, charging him with heresy.

4. What happens to Estienne after his public preaching?

Estienne manages to escape from the soldiers by fleeing into the maze of alleyways surrounding the square.

5. What mysterious invitation does Lucien receive at the end of the chapter?

Lucien finds a note inviting him to a secret meeting at an abandoned chapel at sunset, with the password "sola scriptura."

Scripture Spotlight

1. 2 Timothy 4:2 "Preach the word; be ready in season and out of season; reprove, rebuke, and exhort, with complete patience and teaching."

This verse relates to Estienne's bold preaching in the marketplace, regardless of the consequences.

2. Matthew 10:27 "What I tell you in the dark, say in the light, and what you hear whispered, proclaim on the housetops."

This verse connects with Estienne's fearless public proclamation of his beliefs, despite the danger from authorities.

3. Proverbs 28:1 "The wicked flee when no one pursues, but the righteous are bold as a lion."

This verse reflects both Estienne's courage in speaking out and Lucien's decision to pursue the truth by following the note's instructions, despite the risks involved.

Relevant Topics

1. Have you ever felt torn between speaking out about something you believe in and staying quiet to avoid conflict?

Like Lucien witnessing Estienne's bold speech, you might face situations where you're unsure whether to voice your opinions openly or keep them to yourself. Consider the potential consequences and benefits of speaking out, and think about effective ways to express your views that balance making an impact with maintaining your safety and relationships.

2. How do you verify information you come across, especially when it challenges mainstream ideas?

In this chapter, Lucien and others encounter ideas that contradict the established Church teachings. In your digital age, you're likely exposed to various conflicting information. Develop critical thinking skills, fact-check using reliable sources, and be open to changing your views when presented with credible evidence.

3. Have you ever been invited to join a group or cause that seemed exciting but potentially risky?

Lucien receives a mysterious invitation at the end of the chapter, much like how you might be invited to join online groups or real-world movements. While these can be opportunities for growth and making a difference, they can also pose risks. Evaluate such invitations carefully, considering both the potential benefits and dangers, and don't hesitate to seek advice from trusted adults.

Activities

1. Create a "Secret Message" System:

Develop your own code or cipher inspired by the note Lucien receives. Write a short message about a belief or cause important to you using this code. Exchange coded messages with friends and try to decipher each other's work. Reflect on how this experience relates to the challenges of communicating sensitive information in both historical and modern contexts.

2. Organize a "Marketplace Debate":

Set up a mock marketplace with your friends, assigning roles such as merchants, customers, and a "town crier" (like Estienne). Choose a current controversial topic and have the "town crier" make a public proclamation about it. Other participants should react in character, discussing the proclamation's merits and risks. Afterward, discuss how this simulation compares to modern forms of public discourse, such as social media debates.

3. Write a "Consequences Web":

Draw a diagram starting with Estienne's action of public preaching. Branch out from this central event, listing all the immediate consequences you can think of based on the chapter. Then, for each of these consequences, branch out further to show potential long-term effects. Finally, relate this to your own life by identifying a situation where a single action or decision could have far-reaching consequences. Discuss how this exercise affects your understanding of personal responsibility and decision-making.

CHAPTER 9
The Inquisitor's Shadow

Summary

In this pivotal chapter, Lucien delves deeper into the clandestine world of the Waldensians by attending a secret meeting of The Illuminated in an abandoned chapel. Here, he encounters a diverse group of believers, each with their own harrowing tales of persecution and resilience. The gravity of their situation becomes painfully clear when they learn of Gilbert's capture by the Inquisition, a blow that shakes the group but also reinforces their commitment to their cause. Through shared stories and fervent discussions, Lucien gains a profound understanding of the risks and sacrifices involved in preserving and spreading the forbidden scriptures. The chapter vividly illustrates the constant tension between faith and fear, the importance of community in resistance movements, and the lengths to which believers will go to protect their truth. As the night draws to a close, Estienne's invitation for Lucien to stay with his family underscores the growing bonds within this secret brotherhood, offering a glimmer of warmth amidst the encroaching shadows of the Inquisition.

Key Characters

- Lucien - The protagonist, newly initiated into The Illuminated
- Estienne - A bold young preacher who brings Lucien into the group
- Lazare (God is my helper) - The elder leader of The Illuminated
- Adrienne (dark) - A member who witnessed Gilbert's capture
- Gilbert - Lucien's mentor, now captured by the Inquisition
- Remy (remedy) - A young man who shares a story of a close escape
- Isabelle (devoted to God) - A young woman whose father was taken by the Inquisition

- Thibault (brave people) - A grizzled member who explains the risks of their mission
- Marguerite (daisy) - Adrienne's young sister

Central Themes

1. Faith Under Persecution:

This theme is central to the chapter, exploring how the members of The Illuminated maintain their beliefs in the face of constant danger. The capture of Gilbert and the stories shared by various members highlight the personal costs and risks associated with their faith. It demonstrates how adversity can strengthen conviction and how individuals find courage in their beliefs despite the threat of torture, imprisonment, or death.

2. The Power of Community in Resistance:

The chapter emphasizes the importance of solidarity and mutual support within the secret group. The Illuminated provide each other with emotional support, share resources, and work together to protect their sacred texts and spread their message. This theme illustrates how communities can form and persist under oppressive conditions, providing strength and purpose to their members.

3. Preservation and Dissemination of Truth:

A core theme of the chapter is the group's commitment to preserving and spreading what they believe to be the true word of God. The lengths to which they go to protect the scriptures, develop secret networks, and risk their lives to share their message underscores the power they attribute to these ideas. This theme explores the conflict between established authority and those who challenge it, as well as the lengths people will go to defend and propagate the truth.

Q&A

1. What is the name of the secret group Lucien joins in this chapter?

The group is called The Illuminated.

2. What significant news does Lucien learn about Gilbert during the meeting?

Lucien learns that Gilbert has been captured by the Inquisition and is being held in jail.

3. Who witnessed Gilbert's capture and narrowly escaped?

Adrienne witnessed Gilbert's capture in the marketplace and managed to escape.

4. What method does Isabelle's father use to preserve and share the forbidden scriptures?

Isabelle's father, a scribe, would copy approved texts by day but read from the forbidden scriptures to his family at night.

5. How does the chapter end for Lucien?

The chapter ends with Estienne inviting Lucien to stay the night with his family for safety and companionship.

Scripture Spotlight

1. Romans 8:31 "What then shall we say to these things? If God is for us, who can be against us?"

This verse reflects the group's determination to continue their mission despite the threats they face, embodying their faith in divine protection.

2. 2 Timothy 1:7 "For God gave us a spirit not of fear but of power and love and self-control."

This verse resonates with the courage displayed by The Illuminated members in the face of danger, and their determination to continue their mission despite the risks.

3. Hebrews 10:24-25 "And let us consider how to stir up one another to love and good works, not neglecting to meet together, as is the habit of some, but encouraging one another, and all the more as you see the Day drawing near."

This passage relates to the group's secret meetings and how they draw strength and encouragement from each other in the face of persecution.

Relevant Topics

1. Have you ever been part of a group that shares your beliefs or values, even if those beliefs aren't popular with everyone?

Like The Illuminated, you might find yourself drawn to groups that share your core values or beliefs. These could be religious groups, social justice organizations, or even online communities. Consider how being part of such a group impacts your sense of belonging and purpose, and how it might shape your actions and decisions.

2. How do you support friends or community members who are going through difficult times, similar to how The Illuminated supported each other?

Like The Illuminated rallying around the news of Gilbert's capture, you might face situations where friends or community members are struggling. Consider how you can offer support, whether it's through active listening, offering practical help, or simply being present. Remember that small acts of kindness and solidarity can make a big difference in challenging times.

3. How do you verify information and decide what 'truths' to believe in, especially when faced with conflicting sources?

The Illuminated risked everything for what they believed to be the truth in the scriptures. In your world of instant information and potential misinformation, it's crucial to develop strong critical thinking skills. Learn to cross-reference sources, question the motivations behind information, and be open to changing your views when presented with credible evidence.

Activities

1. Create a Secret Society Simulation:

Organize a group of friends to form a mock secret society inspired by The Illuminated. Develop a mission statement, create secret codes or signals, and assign roles to each member. Over the course of a week, exchange coded messages about a harmless "secret" (like planning a surprise party) while trying to avoid detection by other classmates who act as "Inquisitors." Afterward, discuss the challenges of maintaining secrecy and the impact it had on your communication and relationships.

2. Develop an "Underground Network" Game:

Create a board game that simulates the challenges faced by The Illuminated. Design a map of a medieval city with various locations (safe houses, marketplaces, Inquisition strongholds). Players must move secretly through the city, delivering "scriptures" to specific locations while avoiding capture. Include event cards that present moral dilemmas or unexpected challenges. After playing, discuss how the game reflects real-world scenarios of persecuted groups and the difficult decisions they face.

3. Write and Perform Monologues:

Choose one of the characters from The Illuminated (like Isabelle, Remy, or Thibault) and write a 2-3 minute monologue from their perspective. Dive deep into their backstory, exploring their motivations, fears, and hopes. Perform your monologue for friends or family, staying in character to answer questions afterward. Reflect on how this exercise helps you understand different perspectives and the personal impact of standing up for one's beliefs.

CHAPTER 10
Kindred Spirits

Summary

In this charming chapter, Lucien finds temporary refuge and unexpected kinship with Estienne's family. The warm welcome from Estienne's mother, Madeline, and the engaging interactions with his sister, Orielle, provide Lucien with a brief respite from the dangers of their mission. A shared meal becomes a platform for connection, particularly between Lucien and Orielle, as they excitedly discuss biblical stories and the power of the written word. However, this peaceful interlude is shattered by the arrival of the Inquisition, forcing the family and Lucien to hide in a secret room. The close call serves as a stark reminder of the constant peril they face. Recognizing the danger their presence poses to Estienne's family, Lucien and Estienne make the difficult decision to leave in the night. The chapter concludes with emotional farewells, highlighting the personal sacrifices made in pursuit of their cause and the strength found in unexpected bonds of friendship and faith.

Key Characters

- Lucien - The protagonist, finding brief sanctuary with Estienne's family
- Estienne - Lucien's friend and fellow Waldensian
- Madeline (maiden from Magdala) - Estienne's mother, who warmly welcomes Lucien
- Orielle (golden) - Estienne's younger sister, who bonds with Lucien over their shared love of scriptures
- The Inquisition - Though not individual characters, their presence drives the action in the latter part of the chapter

Central Themes

1. The Power of Found Family and Hospitality:

This theme is central to the chapter, as Lucien experiences warmth, acceptance, and genuine connection within Estienne's family. Despite the dangers and their brief acquaintance, Madeline and Orielle treat Lucien as one of their own, offering him not just physical shelter but emotional refuge as well. This theme highlights how bonds of faith and shared values can create family-like connections even among strangers.

2. The Intersection of Faith and Personal Relationships:

The chapter explores how shared faith can deepen personal relationships, as seen in the bond that quickly forms between Lucien and Orielle over their mutual love for the scriptures. This theme also manifests in the way the family's faith informs their actions, such as their willingness to risk their safety to shelter Lucien.

3. The Constant Tension Between Safety and Mission:

Throughout the chapter, there's an underlying tension between the comfort and safety found in Estienne's home and the dangerous reality of their mission. This culminates in the Inquisition's search and the subsequent decision for Lucien and Estienne to leave. This theme underscores the personal sacrifices required in pursuing their beliefs and the ever-present threat they face.

Q&A

1. Who are the new characters introduced in this chapter?

The new characters introduced are Madeline (Estienne's mother) and Orielle (Estienne's younger sister).

2. What common interest do Lucien and Orielle bond over?

Lucien and Orielle bond over their shared love for scriptures and stories, particularly discussing the Acts of the Apostles.

3. What interrupts the peaceful evening at Estienne's home?

The arrival of the Inquisition, who come to search the house, interrupts the peaceful evening.

4. How does the family escape detection by the Inquisition?

They hide in a secret room within the house until the Inquisition leaves.

5. Why do Lucien and Estienne decide to leave at the end of the chapter?

They decide to leave to protect Estienne's family from the danger their presence brings, recognizing that it's too risky for them to stay after the Inquisition's visit.

Scripture Spotlight

1. Proverbs 17:17 "A friend loves at all times, and a brother is born for adversity."

This verse reflects the bond formed between Lucien and Estienne's family, particularly in the face of danger.

2. Hebrews 13:2 "Do not neglect to show hospitality to strangers, for thereby some have entertained angels unawares."

This verse aligns with Madeline's warm welcome of Lucien into their home, despite the potential risks.

3. Colossians 3:16 "Let the word of Christ dwell in you richly, teaching and admonishing one another in all wisdom, singing psalms and hymns and spiritual songs, with thankfulness in your hearts to God."

This verse aligns with Lucien and Orielle's shared enthusiasm for Scripture and their discussion of biblical stories.

Relevant Topics

1. Have you ever formed a quick, deep connection with someone over a shared interest or belief, like Lucien and Orielle did?

In today's world, you might find yourself connecting with people online or in person over shared passions, be it books, music, or social causes. These connections can form rapidly and feel profound. Consider how these bonds enrich your life and broaden your perspectives, but also be mindful of maintaining healthy boundaries, especially in online interactions.

2. How would you handle a situation where helping a friend might put you or your family at risk?

While you're unlikely to face dangers as extreme as those in the story, you might encounter situations where supporting a friend could have negative consequences for you. This could involve standing up to bullies or reporting concerning behavior. Reflect on your values and the potential outcomes, and don't hesitate to seek advice from trusted adults when facing such dilemmas.

3. In what ways can you create a welcoming and safe space for others, similar to how Estienne's family welcomed Lucien?

In today's diverse society, you might encounter people from different backgrounds or those going through difficult times. Think about how you can make others feel welcome and accepted in your social circles, clubs, or community groups. This could involve simple acts of kindness, standing up against bullying or discrimination, or actively including those who might feel marginalized. Remember that small gestures of inclusion can have a big impact on someone's sense of belonging and safety.

Activities

1. Create a "Safe Haven" Design:

Sketch or design a modern-day "safe haven" inspired by Estienne's family home. Include both visible welcoming elements and hidden safety features. Your design should have at least one secret room or passage. Create a floor plan and write a brief description of how each element contributes to both hospitality and safety. Present your design to friends or family, explaining how it reflects the themes of welcome and protection from the chapter.

2. Organize a "Storytelling Circle":

Gather a group of friends and host a storytelling circle inspired by Lucien and Orielle's discussion. Choose a book, movie, or historical event that everyone is familiar with. Take turns retelling parts of the story from different characters' perspectives. After each retelling, discuss how changing the perspective alters the story's impact. Reflect on how this exercise relates to understanding different viewpoints in real-life situations.

3. Write and Perform "Farewell Letters":

Imagine you're in Lucien or Estienne's position, having to leave loved ones for their safety. Write a heartfelt farewell letter to a family member or close friend, explaining your reasons for leaving and your hopes for the future. Then, write a response letter from the perspective of the person receiving it. Share your letters with a partner and discuss the emotions and challenges involved in making such difficult decisions. Reflect on how this relates to modern situations where people might have to leave their homes for safety or better opportunities.

CHAPTER 11
The Illuminated Path

Summary

In this pivotal chapter, Lucien and Estienne's flight from danger leads them to an unexpected sanctuary. Following a mysterious figure through the winding streets of Grenoble, they discover a hidden garden housing the secret headquarters of the Illuminated. Here, they meet the Sage, the enigmatic leader of the group, who offers them refuge and the promise of deeper understanding. After a much-needed rest, the young men are introduced to the diverse members of the Illuminated, each with their own compelling story of awakening and dedication to the cause. Throughout their interactions, Lucien and Estienne grapple with profound questions about truth, faith, and the risks of challenging established power. The chapter beautifully illustrates the growing sense of belonging and purpose that Lucien feels among these kindred spirits, while also hinting at the challenges and dangers that lie ahead in their quest to spread forbidden knowledge.

Key Characters

- Lucien - The protagonist, seeking truth and purpose
- Estienne - Lucien's friend and fellow seeker
- The Sage (wise) - The mysterious and wise leader of the Illuminated
- Lazare - An old soldier and member of the Illuminated
- Johannes (God is gracious) - A former monk who left the Church to join the Illuminated
- Adela (noble) - A noblewoman who gave up her title to pursue truth with the Illuminated

Central Themes

1. Sanctuary and Refuge:

This theme is embodied in the hidden garden and cottage, which serve as both a physical and metaphorical sanctuary for the Illuminated. It represents the idea that truth-seekers need safe spaces to learn, grow, and connect with like-minded individuals. The contrast between the hostile outside world and the peaceful garden underscores the importance of finding refuge in a challenging environment.

2. The Power of Community in Resistance:

The chapter emphasizes how the diverse members of the Illuminated come together, united by their shared quest for truth. Each character brings unique experiences and skills to the group, illustrating how a strong community can form around shared ideals, even in the face of persecution. This theme highlights the strength found in collective action and mutual support.

3. The Pursuit of Hidden Truth:

Central to the chapter is the idea that truth is often hidden or suppressed by those in power. The Illuminated's dedication to uncovering and spreading this truth, despite the risks, is a driving force for the characters. This theme explores the tension between established dogma and the search for deeper understanding, as well as the personal and societal costs of challenging the status quo.

Q&A

1. Who is the mysterious figure that leads Lucien and Estienne to the hidden garden?

The mysterious figure is revealed to be the Sage, the leader of the Illuminated.

2. What is the significance of the hidden garden?

The hidden garden serves as a sanctuary and headquarters for the Illuminated, symbolizing a place of safety, learning, and enlightenment away from the dangers of the outside world.

3. How does the Sage initially test Lucien and Estienne?

The Sage asks them about their goals and what they are seeking, to understand their motivations for joining the Illuminated.

4. Who are some of the notable members of the Illuminated that Lucien and Estienne meet?

They meet Johannes (a former monk), Adela (a noblewoman who gave up her title), and Lazare (an old soldier).

5. What feeling does Lucien experience by the end of the chapter?

By the end of the chapter, Lucien feels a strong sense of belonging and purpose among the Illuminated, despite feeling physically tired.

Scripture Spotlight

1. Psalm 61:3 "For you have been my refuge, a strong tower against the enemy."

This verse reflects the sanctuary and protection that Lucien and Estienne find with the Illuminated, away from the threats of the Inquisition.

2. Proverbs 27:17 "Iron sharpens iron, and one man sharpens another."

This verse aligns with the theme of community and mutual support among the Illuminated, as they learn from and strengthen each other in their pursuit of truth.

3. Ephesians 5:8-9 "For at one time you were darkness, but now you are light in the Lord. Walk as children of light (for the fruit of light is found in all that is good and right and true)."

This verse resonates with the transformation experienced by members of the Illuminated, like Johannes the former monk, who left their old lives behind to pursue what they believe is true and right.

Relevant Topics

1. Have you ever felt drawn to a group or community that shares your beliefs or values, even if those beliefs aren't mainstream?

Like Lucien and Estienne finding the Illuminated, you might be attracted to groups that align with your core values or interests. This could be anything from environmental activism to a niche hobby community. Consider how being part of such a group impacts your sense of belonging and purpose. Remember to think critically about the group's beliefs and actions, ensuring they align with your personal ethics.

2. In the age of social media and online communities, how do you create "safe spaces" for open discussion and learning?

Just as the Illuminated had their hidden garden, you might seek or create digital or physical spaces where you can freely discuss ideas and learn from others. This could involve private online forums, study groups, or clubs. Think about how you can foster an environment of trust and respect, where people feel safe sharing their thoughts and questions without fear of judgment or reprisal.

3. How do you balance the pursuit of knowledge and truth with the potential risks or consequences in your life?

While you likely don't face the extreme dangers the Illuminated did, standing up for your beliefs or questioning established norms can still have social or personal consequences. Consider how you can educate yourself on important issues, engage in respectful dialogue, and advocate for what you believe in, while also being mindful of your safety and well-being. Remember, it's okay to set boundaries and choose your battles wisely.

Activities

1. Create a "Modern Illuminated" Social Media Campaign:

Design a social media campaign to spread awareness about an important but underrepresented issue you care about. Create a series of posts, each sharing a key fact or insight about your chosen topic. Use creative methods to present the information, such as infographics, short videos, or eye-catching images. Develop a unique hashtag for your campaign. Share your campaign with friends and track its impact. Afterward, reflect on the challenges and benefits of spreading information in the digital age compared to the Illuminated's methods.

2. Organize a "Council of the Illuminated" Role-play:

Gather a group of friends and assign each person a role based on the characters in the chapter (the Sage, Lucien, Estienne, Johannes, Adela, Lazare). Choose a current controversial topic and hold a mock council meeting where each character presents their perspective on the issue. Stay in character as you debate and discuss solutions. Afterward, reflect on how different backgrounds and experiences shaped each character's viewpoint.

3. Develop a "Hidden Knowledge" Scavenger Hunt:

Create a series of clues and puzzles based on a topic you're passionate about (e.g., social media influence, mental health awareness, technology). Hide these clues in books, online, or around your school/neighborhood. Invite friends to participate in solving the puzzles, each one revealing a piece of information about your chosen topic. Conclude with a group discussion about the "hidden knowledge" they uncovered and why it's important.

Reflect on the experience of seeking out and piecing together information, and how it relates to the Illuminated's quest for truth.

CHAPTER 12
The Waldensian Way

Summary

In this chapter, Lucien and Estienne delve deep into the history, beliefs, and practices of the Waldensian movement under the guidance of the Sage and other Illuminated members. They learn about the movement's origins, its survival against persecution, and its core theological principles that stand in stark contrast to the Catholic Church's teachings. As they immerse themselves in study and prayer, the two young men grow increasingly committed to the Waldensian way of life, characterized by simplicity, service, and unwavering faith. The chapter reaches its emotional climax with Lucien's decision to be baptized, a powerful moment that solidifies his commitment to the faith and strengthens his bond with his newfound spiritual family. Throughout their journey of learning and spiritual growth, Lucien and Estienne grapple with complex theological concepts, historical narratives, and the challenges of living a life devoted to truth in a world hostile to their beliefs. The chapter concludes with a poignant reflection on the future of their movement, emphasizing themes of hope, perseverance, and the enduring power of faith.

Key Characters

- Lucien - The protagonist, eagerly learning about Waldensian beliefs and ultimately choosing baptism
- Estienne - Lucien's close friend and fellow learner
- The Sage - The wise leader who teaches them about Waldensian history and beliefs
- Lazare - An older member who passionately critiques Catholic practices

- Remy - Another member of the Illuminated who contributes to
  discussions
- Thibault - A member who shares insights about Waldensian
  practices

Central Themes

1. The Power of Knowledge and Education in Faith:

This theme is central to the chapter, as Lucien and Estienne immerse
themselves in learning about Waldensian history, theology, and practices.
The emphasis on studying scriptures in their original languages and
understanding the historical context of their faith highlights the Waldensian
belief in an informed and intellectually grounded spirituality. This theme
underscores the idea that true faith is not blind but is strengthened through
knowledge and understanding.

2. Rejection of Religious Authority and Tradition:

The chapter extensively explores the Waldensian critique of Catholic
practices and beliefs. This theme is manifested in the discussions about
papal authority, sacraments, and various Catholic doctrines that the
Waldensians reject. It emphasizes the Waldensian commitment to what they
believe is the pure, original Christian faith, uncorrupted by human traditions
and institutional power structures.

3. Personal Transformation and Commitment:

Lucien's journey throughout the chapter, culminating in his decision to be
baptized, embodies this theme. It explores how education and community
support can lead to profound personal transformation and a deepening of
faith. The baptism scene represents a public declaration of this internal
change and commitment to a new way of life, highlighting the
transformative power of faith when it is fully embraced.

Q&A

1. What is the origin of the name "Waldenses" or "People of the Valleys"?

The name comes from the fact that this group lived in the deep valleys between mountain ridges that fanned out from the northern Italian city of Turin.

2. Who was Peter Waldo and what was his role in the Waldensian movement?

Peter Waldo was a wealthy merchant from Lyon who experienced a spiritual awakening. Inspired by Jesus' words to the rich young man, he sold his possessions, gave to the poor, and had the New Testament translated into the local language.

3. What are some of the Catholic Church practices that the Waldensians reject, according to the chapter?

The Waldensians reject beliefs in purgatory, veneration of saints and relics, papal pardons, and the sacraments. They also disagree with the concept of papal authority.

4. What significant personal decision does Lucien make in this chapter?

Lucien decides to be baptized, marking a profound commitment to his newfound faith and the Waldensian way of life.

5. According to the Sage, when did the papacy begin to stray from true Christianity?

The Sage states that the Waldensians believe there has been no true Pope since the days of Sylvester in the fourth century.

Scripture Spotlight

1. 2 Timothy 2:15 "Do your best to present yourself to God as one approved, a worker who has no need to be ashamed, rightly handling the word of truth."

This verse reflects the Waldensian emphasis on studying and correctly interpreting scripture.

2. Matthew 3:13-17 "Then Jesus came from Galilee to the Jordan to be baptized by John. But John tried to deter him, saying, 'I need to be baptized by you, and do you come to me?' Jesus replied, 'Let it be so now; it is proper for us to do this to fulfill all righteousness.' Then John consented. As soon as Jesus was baptized, he went up out of the water. At that moment heaven was opened, and he saw the Spirit of God descending like a dove and alighting on him. And a voice from heaven said, 'This is my Son, whom I love; with him I am well pleased.'"

This passage relates to Lucien's baptism scene, emphasizing the spiritual significance of the act.

3. Acts 17:11 "Now the Berean Jews were of more noble character than those in Thessalonica, for they received the message with great eagerness and examined the Scriptures every day to see if what Paul said was true."

This verse aligns with the Waldensian practice of critically examining religious teachings against scripture, as depicted in the chapter.

Relevant Topics

1. Have you ever questioned the beliefs or traditions you've grown up with, similar to how Lucien explores Waldensian teachings?

Like Lucien, you might find yourself questioning beliefs you've always taken for granted. This is a normal part of growing up and developing your own identity. It's important to approach this process with an open mind, seeking information from reliable sources, and discussing your thoughts with trusted mentors or family members. Remember, questioning doesn't necessarily mean rejecting—it can lead to a deeper, more personal understanding of your beliefs.

2. How do you balance respect for authority with the need to think critically about what you're taught?

The Waldensians rejected many teachings of the established Church, which required great courage. In your life, you'll encounter various authorities—teachers, religious leaders, government officials. While it's important to show respect, it's equally crucial to think critically about what you're told. Develop the habit of fact-checking, seeking multiple perspectives, and forming your own opinions based on evidence.

3. In a world of diverse beliefs and ideologies, how do you stay true to your convictions while respecting others?

Lucien and his friends held firm to their beliefs in a hostile environment. Today, you might find yourself in diverse settings where others hold different beliefs. Strive to maintain your convictions while also respecting others' right to their own beliefs. Practice active listening, engage in respectful dialogue, and look for common ground. Remember that it's possible to disagree with someone's ideas without disrespecting them as a person.

Activities

1. Create a Historical Timeline:

Research and create a detailed timeline of the Waldensian movement from its origins to the present day. Include key events, figures, and theological developments mentioned in the chapter. Use a large piece of paper or a digital tool to visually represent your timeline. Add images, quotes, or short explanations for each entry. Present your timeline to friends or family, explaining the significance of each event in the Waldensian story.

2. Organize a "Beliefs Debate":

Set up a structured debate with friends, focusing on one of the theological differences between the Waldensians and the Catholic Church mentioned in the chapter (e.g., the authority of the Pope, the concept of purgatory, or the veneration of saints). Divide into two teams, with one side representing the Waldensian view and the other the Catholic view. Research your assigned position thoroughly, even if it doesn't align with your personal beliefs. After the debate, discuss as a group how this exercise helped you understand different perspectives on religious issues.

3. Conduct a "Sacred Text Translation" Exercise:

Choose a short passage from the Bible that's meaningful to you. Translate this passage into at least three different forms: a visual representation (like a painting or collage), a song or poem, and a modern paraphrase using current slang or technology references. The goal is to make the passage's meaning accessible to different audiences, much like the Waldensians sought to make scripture accessible in local languages. Share your translations with friends or family, discussing how the meaning changes or remains consistent across different forms of expression. Reflect on the challenges and importance of making profound ideas understandable to diverse audiences.

CHAPTER 13
Betrayal in the Valleys

Summary

In this gripping chapter, the Waldensian refuge is shattered by betrayal as Adrienne, once a trusted member, leads the Inquisition to their doorstep. Lucien, Estienne, and their companions are forced to flee into the treacherous mountain terrain, guided by the Sage's wisdom and a mysterious map to a hidden scriptorium. For days, they navigate perilous paths and endure harsh conditions, their resolve tested at every turn. The chapter reaches its climax with a harrowing ambush in a narrow gorge, where the group is scattered, and some members are captured by the Inquisition. Lucien and Estienne manage a narrow escape, but find themselves isolated from their companions. Despite the overwhelming odds and the weight of betrayal, the chapter concludes with the two friends reaffirming their commitment to each other and their cause, embodying the unquenchable spirit of hope that defines their faith.

Key Characters

- Lucien - The protagonist, demonstrating resilience and unwavering friendship
- Estienne - Lucien's loyal friend and fellow fugitive
- The Sage - The wise leader providing guidance and the map
- Lazare - The old soldier who brings news of the betrayal and is later captured
- Adrienne - The unexpected traitor who betrays the group to the Inquisition
- Remy - Another member of the group who is captured during the ambush

Central Themes

Betrayal and Trust:

This theme is central to the chapter, embodied by Adrienne's unexpected betrayal of the group to the Inquisition. It explores the devastating impact of betrayal on a tight-knit community and raises questions about the nature of trust in times of persecution. The theme challenges the characters' assumptions about their relationships and forces them to confront the reality that even those closest to them can become threats.

Perseverance in the Face of Adversity:

Throughout the chapter, the characters demonstrate remarkable resilience as they flee from the Inquisition, navigate treacherous mountain terrain, and endure physical and emotional hardships. This theme is particularly evident in Lucien and Estienne's determination to continue their fight even after being separated from their group and witnessing the capture of their friends.

The Strength of Brotherhood and Faith:

The bond between Lucien and Estienne serves as a powerful illustration of this theme. Their unwavering support for each other, even in the direst circumstances, showcases the strength that can be drawn from deep friendship and shared beliefs. This theme is further reinforced by the group's collective reliance on their faith to sustain them through their trials, emphasizing the power of spiritual conviction in the face of physical danger.

Q&A

1. Who betrays the Waldensian group to the Inquisition?

Adrienne, who was previously a trusted member of their community, betrays the group.

2. What special item does the Sage give to Lucien and Estienne?

The Sage gives them a faded map leading to a scriptorium in the heart of the mountains.

3. How long do Lucien and his companions travel before they are ambushed by the Inquisition?

They travel for five days before being ambushed while crossing a narrow gorge.

4. What happens to Lazare and Remy during the ambush?

Lazare is wounded and falls, while Remy is dragged from his horse and captured by the Inquisition.

5. How does the chapter end for Lucien and Estienne?

The chapter ends with Lucien and Estienne exhausted but determined, reaffirming their commitment to each other and their cause as they set off into the darkness.

Scripture Spotlight

Romans 8:35,37 "Who shall separate us from the love of Christ? Shall tribulation, or distress, or persecution, or famine, or nakedness, or danger, or sword?... No, in all these things we are more than conquerors through him who loved us."

This verse reflects the perseverance of Lucien and Estienne in the face of extreme adversity and persecution.

Psalm 55:12-14 "For it is not an enemy who taunts me—then I could bear it; it is not an adversary who deals insolently with me—then I could hide from him. But it is you, a man, my equal, my companion, my familiar friend."

This passage relates to the theme of betrayal, particularly Adrienne's betrayal of the group, which is especially painful because it comes from someone they trusted.

Proverbs 18:24 "A man of many companions may come to ruin, but there is a friend who sticks closer than a brother."

This verse aligns with the strong bond between Lucien and Estienne, highlighting their unwavering friendship and support for each other throughout their trials.

Relevant Topics

1. Have you ever experienced betrayal from someone you trusted, and how did you handle it?

Like Lucien and his friends, you might have faced betrayal from someone close to you. While it's unlikely to be as extreme as in the story, betrayal in friendships or relationships can be deeply hurtful. Remember that it's okay to feel hurt and angry, but try not to let it destroy your ability to trust others. Learn from the experience, seek support from true friends, and focus on moving forward positively.

2. How do you maintain hope and determination when facing seemingly insurmountable challenges?

Lucien and Estienne demonstrate remarkable resilience in the face of extreme adversity. In your life, you might face challenges that feel overwhelming—perhaps academic pressure, family issues, or social difficulties. Like the characters, try to draw strength from your support system, whether it's friends, family, or mentors. Set small, achievable goals, celebrate small victories, and remind yourself of your inner strength and past successes.

3. In times of crisis, how do you decide when to stand and fight, and when to retreat and regroup?

Lucien and Estienne have to make quick decisions about when to flee and when to stand their ground. While you're unlikely to face life-threatening situations, you might encounter conflicts or challenges where you need to decide whether to confront an issue head-on or step back temporarily. Consider the potential consequences of your actions, assess whether you have the resources and support to face the challenge, and think about long-term goals versus short-term gains. Sometimes, like the characters in the story, a strategic retreat can be the wisest course of action.

Activities

1. Create a "Trust Network" Map:

Draw a diagram of your personal "trust network." Place yourself at the center and map out your relationships with family, friends, mentors, and acquaintances. Use different colors or line styles to represent levels of trust. Then, write a short reflection on why you trust certain people more than others. Consider how you would rebuild trust if it were broken, inspired by the Waldensians' experience with betrayal. Share your map with a trusted friend or family member and discuss strategies for maintaining and strengthening trust in relationships.

2. Design an "Escape and Evade" Strategy Game:

Create a board game or smartphone app based on the Waldensians' flight from the Inquisition. Design a map with various terrains (mountains, forests, villages) and challenges (Inquisition patrols, natural obstacles, resource scarcity). Develop rules for movement, hiding, and resource management. Include cards for unexpected events, both positive (finding allies) and negative (betrayals). Play your game with friends and discuss how it relates to real-world situations where people face persecution or need to make difficult decisions under pressure.

3. Create a "Survival Skills Workshop":

Organize a practical workshop to learn and practice survival skills inspired by the Waldensians' journey through the mountains. Research and demonstrate techniques such as building a shelter, finding and purifying water, identifying edible plants, and basic first aid. Create a series of challenges for your friends to complete, such as starting a fire without matches or navigating using natural landmarks. Discuss how these skills relate to modern-day emergency preparedness and outdoor safety. Reflect on the resourcefulness and resilience required in survival situations, both in the story and in real life.

CHAPTER 14
The Scriptorium's Sanctuary

Summary

In this chapter, Lucien and Estienne's harrowing journey culminates in the discovery of the hidden Scriptorium Valdese, a sanctuary deep within the mountains. Guided by the Sage's cryptic final instructions and a faded map, they uncover a secret entrance marked with the Waldensian symbol. Using a clever combination of password and rhythmic knocking, they gain access to an underground marvel—a vast chamber filled with scribes diligently preserving sacred texts. Here, they meet Jerome, the keeper of the scriptorium, who welcomes them and explains the sanctuary's long history of evading the Inquisition through ingenious concealment techniques. As Lucien and Estienne settle into their new roles as scribes, they find a deep sense of purpose in continuing the Waldensian legacy, despite their lingering concerns for their fallen comrades. The chapter beautifully intertwines themes of faith, perseverance, and the power of knowledge preservation in the face of relentless persecution.

Key Characters

- Lucien - The protagonist, who helps discover the scriptorium's entrance
- Estienne - Lucien's loyal friend and fellow fugitive
- Jerome (sacred name) - The elderly keeper of the Scriptorium Valdese
- The Sage - Though not present, his guidance is crucial to finding the scriptorium
- The young lad - A silent guide who leads Lucien and Estienne into the scriptorium

Central Themes

1. The Power of Hidden Knowledge and Preservation:

This theme is central to the chapter, embodied by the secret scriptorium and its centuries-long mission to preserve Waldensian texts. The elaborate measures taken to conceal and protect this repository of knowledge underscore its immense value. It highlights how persecuted groups throughout history have gone to great lengths to safeguard their beliefs and cultural heritage, often through clandestine means.

2. Faith and Perseverance in the Face of Adversity:

Lucien and Estienne's arduous journey to find the scriptorium, guided only by cryptic instructions and unwavering faith, exemplifies this theme. Their determination to continue the Waldensian mission, even after facing betrayal and near-capture, demonstrates the resilience of their beliefs. The scriptorium itself stands as a testament to generations of faithful individuals persevering against ongoing threats.

3. Ingenuity as a Tool of Resistance:

The intricate mechanisms used to conceal and protect the scriptorium—from the hidden entrance to the clever warning system—highlight how innovation and creativity can be powerful tools for resisting oppression. This theme explores how marginalized groups often develop sophisticated methods to preserve their way of life, using intellect and resourcefulness to counteract the brute force of their persecutors.

Q&A

1. What is the secret phrase used to gain entry to the scriptorium?

The phrase is "Sola scriptura, Amen," which is knocked on the rock in a specific rhythm rather than spoken aloud.

2. Who is Jerome and what is his role?

Jerome is the elderly keeper of the Scriptorium Valdese, responsible for maintaining the sanctuary and guiding new arrivals.

3. How has the scriptorium remained hidden from the Inquisition for so long?

The scriptorium uses multiple hidden entrances, each with a unique key, and employs clever mechanisms like false stone facades and hidden warning systems.

4. What symbol marks the entrance to the scriptorium?

The entrance is marked with the Waldensian symbol of a flame and a book, representing the eternal light of truth.

5. What is the primary activity taking place in the scriptorium?

The main activity is the transcription and preservation of sacred texts by scribes of various ages, working to maintain Waldensian knowledge.

Scripture Spotlight

1. Psalm 27:5 "For he will hide me in his shelter in the day of trouble; he will conceal me under the cover of his tent; he will lift me high upon a rock."

This verse reflects the sanctuary and protection that Lucien and Estienne find in the hidden scriptorium.

2. Proverbs 2:6-7 "For the Lord gives wisdom; from his mouth come knowledge and understanding; he stores up sound wisdom for the upright; he is a shield to those who walk in integrity."

This passage relates to the preservation of knowledge in the scriptorium and the protection provided to those seeking truth.

3. Colossians 3:16 "Let the word of Christ dwell in you richly, teaching and admonishing one another in all wisdom, singing psalms and hymns and spiritual songs, with thankfulness in your hearts to God."

This passage aligns with the activities in the scriptorium, where scribes are dedicated to preserving and sharing the word of God. It also reflects the sense of community and shared purpose that Lucien and Estienne find in their new roles.

Relevant Topics

1. In an age of digital information, how can you contribute to preserving important knowledge or cultural heritage?

Like the scribes in the scriptorium, you can play a role in preserving knowledge. Consider digitizing old family photos or documents, contributing to online wikis about your local history, or learning and sharing traditional skills or stories from your culture. Remember, preservation isn't just about old texts—it's about keeping important information and traditions alive for future generations.

2. How can you use technology and innovation to protect your privacy and personal information in the digital age?

Just as the Waldensians used clever mechanisms to protect their sanctuary, you can employ modern tools to safeguard your digital life. Consider using strong, unique passwords for different accounts, enabling two-factor authentication, being cautious about what you share on social media, and learning about encryption for sensitive communications. Before you click or tap on links in your emails and text messages, make sure they come from authentic sources. Be wary of phishing attempts and unsolicited messages asking for personal information. Additionally, regularly update your devices and applications to ensure you have the latest security features. Remember, in the digital world, vigilance is key to maintaining your privacy and security.

3. In what ways can you create a "sanctuary" for yourself or others in challenging times?

The scriptorium provided both physical safety and spiritual comfort. In your life, creating a sanctuary might mean designating a quiet space for reflection or study, fostering a supportive friend group, or developing coping mechanisms for stress. Think about what makes you feel safe and centered, and try to incorporate those elements into your daily life. Remember, a sanctuary can be a state of mind as much as a physical place.

Activities

1. Design a "Hidden in Plain Sight" Device:

Create a clever hiding place for a small, valuable object (like a USB drive or a note) inspired by the scriptorium's hidden entrance. Use everyday items to construct a concealment that appears innocuous but contains a secret compartment. Consider incorporating a puzzle or mechanism that must be solved to access the hidden area. Present your creation to friends or family, challenging them to find the hidden object. Discuss how this exercise relates to the need for protecting important information in both historical and modern contexts.

2. Host a "Scribes' Workshop":

Organize a calligraphy or hand-lettering session with friends. Research different historical scripts and choose one to practice. Use pens, ink, or even quills if available. Create short passages from favorite books or meaningful quotes, focusing on the meditative aspect of carefully forming each letter. As you work, discuss the value of handwriting in a digital age and the role of scribes in preserving knowledge throughout history. Consider how the act of slowly writing out a text changes your relationship with the words. Conclude by reflecting on the dedication of the scribes in the chapter and how their work relates to modern forms of information preservation.

3. Organize "A Day in a Copyist's Life" Event:

Plan and host an event where participants experience the role of medieval copyists. Have volunteers hand-write portions of Scripture, such as a complete book of the Bible or sections of the New Testament. Divide the text among participants, providing guidelines for consistent formatting and style. Use materials that mimic historical practices, like quills and parchment-like paper, if possible. After completion, work together to bind the pages into a cohesive document. Consider donating the finished product to a local church, community organization, or museum. Conclude the event with a group discussion, reflecting on the experience of engaging with the text in this hands-on way. Explore the challenges faced by historical copyists and discuss the significance of hand-copied scriptures in preserving and spreading sacred texts throughout history.

CHAPTER 15
A Risky Rendezvous

Summary

In this gripping chapter, Lucien and Estienne's life in the scriptorium takes a dramatic turn as they balance their duties as scribes with intense combat training. Their peaceful routine is shattered when Jerome delivers devastating news: Lazare and Remy have died, the Sage has been captured, and the Inquisition looms nearby. Tasked with a perilous mission to meet Philippe from an outpost, the pair embarks on a treacherous journey through mountainous terrain. Their encounter with Philippe reveals a chilling truth—Adrienne, their former ally, may have betrayed them to the Inquisition. As they grapple with this betrayal and the imminent threat to their sanctuary, Lucien and Estienne must steel themselves for a dangerous plan to thwart their enemies. The chapter masterfully weaves themes of faith, loyalty, and sacrifice, highlighting the personal costs of their relentless pursuit of truth in a world fraught with danger.

Key Characters

- Lucien - The protagonist, evolving from scribe to potential warrior
- Estienne - Lucien's steadfast companion and fellow trainee
- Jerome - The wise leader of the scriptorium who assigns the mission
- Marcel (little warrior) - The gruff combat instructor
- Philippe (lover of horses) - The outpost leader who provides crucial intelligence
- Adrienne - The suspected traitor, though not physically present
- The Sage - Mentioned as captured, his fate weighs heavily on the others

Central Themes

1. The Balance Between Preservation and Action:

This theme is central to the chapter, as Lucien and Estienne transition from their roles as scribes to potential warriors. It explores the idea that protecting truth sometimes requires more than just preserving knowledge; it may demand physical action and sacrifice. The juxtaposition of their scribal duties with combat training highlights the multifaceted nature of their mission and the complex demands of their faith in dangerous times.

2. Betrayal and Its Consequences:

The revelation of Adrienne's suspected betrayal underscores this theme. It explores the devastating impact of treachery on a close-knit community and the painful decisions it forces upon the remaining faithful. This theme also touches on the psychological toll of suspicion and the challenge of maintaining trust in a world where loyalties can shift unexpectedly.

3. Faith Tested Through Adversity:

Throughout the chapter, the characters' faith is constantly challenged by dire circumstances. From the loss of comrades to the looming threat of the Inquisition, Lucien and Estienne must repeatedly choose to persevere in their beliefs despite mounting obstacles. This theme explores how adversity can either strengthen or break one's faith, and how religious conviction can provide strength in the face of seemingly insurmountable odds.

Q&A

1. What new skills are Lucien and Estienne learning at the scriptorium besides scribal work?

They are learning combat skills, including archery and swordplay, under the instruction of Marcel.

2. What tragic news does Jerome share with Lucien and Estienne?

Jerome informs them that Lazare and Remy died in an ambush, the Sage has been captured, and the Inquisition is camped nearby.

3. What is the password Lucien and Estienne must use to identify themselves to Philippe and what does it mean?

The password is "Lux Lucet in Tenebris," which means "light shining in the darkness."

4. Who does Philippe suspect the Inquisition is waiting for, and why is this significant?

Philippe suspects they're waiting for Adrienne, who they believe may have betrayed the Waldensians by agreeing to share information about the scriptorium's location.

5. What internal conflict does Lucien face when considering the possibility of confronting Adrienne?

Lucien struggles with the idea of potentially having to harm Adrienne, who was once their friend and fellow believer, in order to protect the scriptorium and their cause.

Scripture Spotlight

1. John 15:13 "Greater love has no one than this, that someone lay down his life for his friends."

Lucien and Estienne's willingness to risk their lives to protect the scriptorium and their fellow Waldensians embodies this sacrificial love.

2. Romans 8:28 "And we know that for those who love God all things work together for good, for those who are called according to his purpose."

Despite the betrayal by Adrienne and the looming confrontation, this verse affirms that God can bring good even out of difficult circumstances for those who are faithful.

3. Psalm 31:14-15 "But I trust in you, O Lord; I say, 'You are my God.' My times are in your hand; rescue me from the hand of my enemies and from my persecutors!"

This verse reflects the characters' unwavering faith in the face of persecution and danger, particularly as they confront the threat of the Inquisition.

Relevant Topics

1. How do you balance acquiring knowledge with developing practical skills in your life?

Like Lucien and Estienne, who combine scribal work with combat training, you might find yourself needing to balance academic learning with practical skills. Consider how you can complement your studies with real-world experiences, internships, or vocational training. Remember that a well-rounded education often involves both theoretical knowledge and hands-on skills.

2. How do you maintain your personal beliefs or values when they're challenged by societal pressures or opposing viewpoints?

Like the Waldensians who held onto their faith despite persecution, you might face situations where your beliefs or values are challenged by peers, social media, or societal norms. Reflect on why you hold these beliefs, be open to respectful dialogue with those who disagree, and seek out supportive communities that share your values. Remember, standing firm in your convictions often requires courage and a willingness to critically examine both your own views and those of others.

3. In what ways can you prepare yourself to face unexpected challenges or crises in your life?

Lucien and Estienne undergo combat training to prepare for potential threats. While you're unlikely to need such extreme skills, you can prepare for life's challenges in various ways:

- *Develop good study and time management habits*
- *Learn stress management and coping techniques*
- *Build a strong support network of friends, family, and mentors*
- *Acquire basic first aid skills*
- *Consider taking a self-defense course for personal safety*
- *Practice problem-solving and critical thinking skills*
- *Develop financial literacy and basic budgeting skills*
- *Learn basic cooking and household management*
- *Stay informed about current events and potential societal changes*
- *Cultivate resilience through the study of your Bible and developing a relationship with Jesus-Christ*

Reflect on the potential challenges you might face in the near future and identify specific steps you can take now to be better prepared. Remember, preparation is not about anticipating every possible scenario, but about developing a flexible, resilient mindset to handle unexpected situations.

Activities

1. Organize an "Ethical Dilemma" Debate:

Set up a structured debate focusing on the moral challenges presented in the chapter, such as "Is betraying your group ever justified?" or "How far should one go to protect their beliefs?" Divide into teams, with each side presenting arguments for their assigned position, even if it doesn't align with personal views. Use examples from history or current events to support your arguments. After the debate, discuss as a group how this exercise helped you understand the complexity of moral decisions in difficult situations. Reflect on how you might apply this kind of critical thinking to ethical challenges in your own life.

2. Conduct a "Dual Skills" Challenge:

Organize a competition that combines intellectual and physical tasks, mirroring Lucien and Estienne's balance of scribal work and combat training. Create stations with activities like solving riddles while maintaining a plank position, memorizing a passage while juggling, or completing a puzzle while walking on a balance beam. Challenge yourself and your friends to excel in both types of tasks. Reflect on the importance of developing a well-rounded skill set and how different abilities can complement each other in unexpected ways.

3. Organize a "Preserve the Knowledge" Challenge:

Choose an aspect of your local culture, history, or environment that you believe is important to preserve. Research this topic thoroughly, then create a time capsule that effectively captures this knowledge. Use a combination of written documents, photos, and small artifacts. Write a guide explaining the significance of each item and how future generations might use this information. Present your time capsule to friends or family, explaining your choices and the importance of preserving this knowledge. Discuss how this exercise relates to the scribes' work in the chapter and the modern challenges of preserving cultural heritage.

CHAPTER 16
The Prisoner's Plight

Summary

In this intense chapter, Lucien and Estienne's plan to intercept Adrienne takes a devastating turn. As they confront her, they discover the heart-wrenching reason behind her betrayal—the Inquisition's capture of her young sister, Marguerite. Before they can formulate a rescue plan, Inquisition forces ambush them, leading to a fierce but ultimately futile battle. The chapter reaches its climax with Estienne gravely wounded and Lucien captured, while Adrienne's fate hangs in the balance. Throughout the conflict, the characters grapple with impossible choices between loyalty, family, and faith. Lucien's capture marks a turning point, as he silently vows to save both Estienne and Marguerite, clinging to his faith even as he faces the terror of imprisonment by the Inquisition. The chapter powerfully illustrates the personal cost of their struggle and the strength drawn from unwavering belief in the face of overwhelming adversity.

Key Characters

- Lucien - The protagonist, captured by the Inquisition
- Estienne - Lucien's close friend, seriously wounded in the battle
- Adrienne - The conflicted betrayer, coerced by the Inquisition
- Marguerite - Adrienne's sister, held hostage by the Inquisition (mentioned but not present)
- The Inquisitor - Leader of the ambushing forces
- Philippe - Mentioned as the creator of the map (not present in the main action)

Central Themes

1. Moral Dilemmas and Impossible Choices:

This theme is central to the chapter, embodied in Adrienne's decision to betray her comrades to save her sister, and in Lucien and Estienne's struggle to balance their loyalty to the Waldensian cause with their desire to save an innocent child. It explores the complexity of moral decisions in extreme circumstances, where there are no clear-cut right answers and every choice comes with a heavy cost.

2. Faith and Resilience in the Face of Adversity:

Throughout the chapter, characters draw strength from their faith to confront seemingly insurmountable challenges. This is particularly evident in Lucien's recitation of Psalm 23:4 as he's being taken captive, illustrating how belief can provide comfort and resolve even in the darkest moments. The theme underscores the power of faith as a source of resilience and hope.

3. The Personal Cost of Ideological Conflict:

The chapter vividly portrays the human toll of the conflict between the Waldensians and the Inquisition. From Adrienne's anguish over her sister to Estienne's wounding and Lucien's capture, it highlights how ideological battles often exact a deeply personal price. This theme explores the tension between abstract beliefs and the very real, often painful consequences for individuals caught in the crossfire of larger conflicts.

Q&A

1. What was Lucien and Estienne's original plan regarding Adrienne?

They planned to intercept Adrienne before she could reach the Inquisition camp, with the intention to capture her if possible or silence her if necessary.

2. Why did Adrienne betray the Waldensians to the Inquisition?

Adrienne was coerced into betraying them because the Inquisition was holding her younger sister, Marguerite, hostage and threatening to torture her.

3. How does the confrontation with Adrienne end unexpectedly?

The confrontation is interrupted by an ambush from Inquisition soldiers, who outnumber and overwhelm Lucien's group.

4. What happens to Estienne during the battle?

Estienne is seriously wounded, with a sword finding a gap in his armor and piercing his side.

5. What vow does Lucien make as he's being captured?

Lucien silently vows to find a way to save both Estienne and Marguerite, despite his own capture.

Scripture Spotlight

1. Psalm 23:4 "Even though I walk through the valley of the shadow of death, I will fear no evil, for you are with me; your rod and your staff, they comfort me."

This verse reflects Lucien's faith and resilience in the face of capture and uncertain fate.

2. Proverbs 3:5-6 "Trust in the Lord with all your heart, and do not lean on your own understanding. In all your ways acknowledge him, and he will make straight your paths."

This passage relates to the characters' struggle to understand and navigate the complex moral dilemmas they face.

3. Romans 8:38-39 "For I am sure that neither death nor life, nor angels nor rulers, nor things present nor things to come, nor powers, nor height nor depth, nor anything else in all creation, will be able to separate us from the love of God in Christ Jesus our Lord."

This verse aligns with the theme of unwavering faith despite severe adversity, mirroring Lucien's determination to hold onto his beliefs even as he's taken captive.

Relevant Topics

1. Have you ever faced a situation where you felt forced to choose between loyalty to your friends and protecting your family?

While your situation may not be as extreme as Adrienne's, you might encounter conflicts between friendships and family obligations. Consider how you would handle such a dilemma. Remember that communication is often key in resolving these conflicts, and don't be afraid to seek advice from trusted adults or mentors when faced with difficult choices.

2. How do you maintain your personal beliefs or values when they're challenged by peer pressure or authority figures?

Like Lucien holding onto his faith while captured, you might face situations where your beliefs are tested. Reflect on what your core values are and why they're important to you. Develop strategies to stay true to yourself, such as surrounding yourself with supportive friends or finding mentors who share your values. Remember, it's okay to respectfully disagree with others, even those in positions of authority.

3. How do you cope with feelings of helplessness when faced with situations that seem beyond your control?

Like Lucien witnessing Estienne's injury and being unable to help, you might encounter situations where you feel powerless. It's important to recognize that some things are out of your control. Focus on what you can influence, seek support from friends and family, and don't hesitate to talk to a counselor or trusted adult if you're feeling overwhelmed. Remember that it's okay to have these feelings, and that seeking help is a sign of strength, not weakness.

Activities

1. Create an "Ethical Dilemma" Role-Play:

Organize a role-playing scenario based on the moral dilemmas in the chapter. Assign roles such as Lucien, Estienne, Adrienne, and the Inquisitor. Create a script with multiple decision points where players must make difficult choices. After the role-play, lead a group discussion about the decisions made, their consequences, and how they relate to real-life ethical dilemmas. Reflect on how you would handle similar situations in your own life and what principles guide your decision-making.

2. Conduct a "Faith Under Fire" Interview Project:

Research historical or contemporary figures who maintained their beliefs despite persecution or extreme adversity. Prepare a series of interview questions as if you could speak to these individuals. With a partner, take turns role-playing as the interviewer and the historical figure. Focus on how they maintained their faith or principles in difficult circumstances. After the interviews, discuss how their experiences compare to those of the characters in the chapter. Consider how you can apply their strength and resilience to challenges in your own life.

3. Create a "Symbols of Hope" Art Installation:

Inspired by Lucien's recitation of Psalm 23:4, design and create an art piece that represents hope in dark times. This could be a painting, sculpture, digital artwork, or mixed media installation. Incorporate symbols or imagery that reflect themes of faith, resilience, and perseverance from the chapter. Present your artwork to a group, explaining the symbolism and how it relates to both the story and your personal experiences. Discuss how art can be a powerful medium for expressing complex emotions and ideas, especially in challenging times.

CHAPTER 17
Estienne's Crucible

Summary

In this harrowing chapter, Lucien endures brutal torture at the hands of the Inquisition, clinging desperately to his faith through recitation of prayers. His resolve is tested to its limits when he glimpses a severely injured Estienne being dragged past his cell. The narrative takes a dramatic turn when Estienne later approaches Lucien, revealing the Inquisitor's tempting offer: recant his faith to save both his own life and his sister Orielle's freedom. Lucien initially proposes a daring plan of false recantation to undermine the Inquisition from within, but quickly realizes the faithlessness of such scheming. In a powerful moment of spiritual recommitment, both men reject human cunning in favor of trusting in God's plan. The chapter concludes with Lucien and Estienne kneeling in prayer, their brotherhood and faith renewed in the face of their dire circumstances. Throughout, the narrative explores profound themes of faith under extreme duress, the temptation to compromise beliefs for loved ones, and the sustaining power of prayer and fraternal bonds in the darkest of times.

Key Characters

- Lucien - The protagonist, enduring torture while maintaining his faith
- Estienne - Lucien's close friend, tempted to recant his faith to save his sister
- Orielle - Estienne's sister, arrested by the Inquisition
- The Inquisitors - The torturers, representing the antagonistic force
- God - Though not a physical character, His presence is central to the characters' faith and decisions

Central Themes

1. Faith Under Extreme Duress:

This theme is central to the chapter, as both Lucien and Estienne face unimaginable physical and psychological torture. Their struggle to maintain their beliefs in the face of excruciating pain and tempting offers of relief demonstrates the depth of their faith. The chapter explores how faith can be both a source of strength and a cause of anguish when it's tested to its limits.

2. The Temptation of Compromise:

The chapter delves deep into the moral dilemma of compromising one's beliefs to protect loved ones. Estienne's temptation to recant his faith to save his sister Orielle represents a poignant exploration of this theme. It raises questions about the nature of faith, the limits of personal sacrifice, and the complex interplay between familial love and spiritual conviction.

3. The Power of Brotherhood and Shared Faith:

Throughout their ordeal, Lucien and Estienne draw strength from their bond as brothers in faith. Their ability to support and uplift each other, even in their darkest moments, highlights the importance of community in maintaining faith and hope. The chapter culminates in their joint recommitment to their beliefs, emphasizing how shared faith can provide resilience in the face of overwhelming adversity.

Q&A

1. What prayer does Lucien repeatedly recite to maintain his faith during torture?

Lucien recites the Lord's Prayer (Our Father) to maintain his faith and endure the torture.

2. What deal does the Inquisitor offer Estienne?

The Inquisitor offers to spare Estienne's life and free his sister Orielle if he recants his faith and denounces the Waldensians.

3. What initial plan does Lucien suggest to Estienne to escape their situation?

Lucien suggests that Estienne pretend to recant, gain the Inquisitors' trust, and then use that position to bring down the Inquisition from within.

4. Why does Lucien suddenly reject his own plan?

Lucien realizes that their scheme relies on their own cunning rather than faith in God, and he sees this as faithless and arrogant.

5. How do Lucien and Estienne ultimately decide to face their ordeal?

They decide to wait on the Lord, pray, and endure, trusting in God's plan rather than their own schemes.

Scripture Spotlight

1. Matthew 6:9-13 "Our Father in heaven, hallowed be your name. Your kingdom come, your will be done, on earth as it is in heaven. Give us this day our daily bread, and forgive us our debts, as we also have forgiven our debtors. And lead us not into temptation, but deliver us from evil."

This prayer is recited repeatedly by Lucien throughout his torture, serving as his lifeline and source of strength.

2. Psalm 22:1 "My God, my God, why have you forsaken me? Why are you so far from saving me, from the words of my groaning?"

This verse reflects Lucien's moment of despair when he cries out, questioning why God has forsaken him, mirroring his feelings of abandonment during intense suffering.

3. Acts 16:25 "About midnight Paul and Silas were praying and singing hymns to God, and the prisoners were listening to them."

This verse parallels Lucien and Estienne's situation, as they, like Paul and Silas, pray and maintain their faith while imprisoned.

4. Isaiah 40:31 "But they who wait for the Lord shall renew their strength; they shall mount up with wings like eagles; they shall run and not be weary; they shall walk and not faint."

This verse corresponds to Lucien and Estienne's final decision to wait on the Lord, trusting that their strength will be renewed through faith and patience.

Relevant Topics

1. How do you find strength or comfort when going through difficult times?

Like Lucien reciting the Lord's Prayer, you might have practices, prayers, or beliefs that help you cope with stress or hardship. Reflect on what gives you strength during tough times.

2. Have you ever realized that a plan you thought was good was actually misguided?

Lucien's sudden realization about their escape plan reflects how our perspectives can quickly change. Reflect on times when you've had to reassess your actions or decisions.

3. In a world of quick fixes and instant gratification, how do you practice patience and trust in long-term outcomes?

Lucien and Estienne's decision to "wait on the Lord" contrasts with the urge for immediate solutions. Think about how you balance immediate action with patience and trust in your life.

Activities

1. Organize a "Trust Fall" Team-Building Exercise:

Set up a safe environment for trust falls or other team-building activities that require faith in others. Participate with a group of friends. Discuss how trusting others and being trustworthy relates to faith and community in challenging times.

2. Host a "Patience Challenge" Week:

Create a week-long challenge where you and your friends practice patience in various ways (e.g., delayed gratification, listening without interrupting). Keep a journal of your experiences. At the end of the week, discuss how practicing patience affected your daily life and decision-making.

3. Develop a "Support Network" Map:

Draw a visual representation of your support network. Include friends, family, mentors, and community resources. Identify areas where your network could be strengthened. Create a plan to build and maintain these supportive relationships. Share your map with a trusted friend or family member and discuss the importance of community in facing life's challenges.

CHAPTER 18
The Copyist's Confession

Summary

In this emotionally charged chapter, Lucien's parents, Simon and Odette, launch a desperate rescue mission upon learning of their son's arrest by the Inquisition. With the aid of Guillaume, a wealthy relative, they manage to bribe guards and free not only Lucien but also his friends Estienne and Orielle from the dungeons. The narrative shifts to a poignant reunion at an inn, where Lucien finally reveals his involvement with the Waldensians to his family. The arrival of Estienne and Orielle's mother adds another layer of emotional depth as the families grapple with the reality of their children's dangerous faith. As the gravity of their situation becomes clear, plans are made for the young people to seek refuge in Switzerland. The chapter culminates in heart-wrenching farewells, with Simon providing Lucien financial support for the journey ahead and reaffirming his unconditional love. Throughout, the story explores themes of familial bonds, sacrifice, unwavering faith, and the profound choices faced by those persecuted for their beliefs, painting a vivid picture of the personal cost of religious conviction in a time of intense persecution.

Key Characters

- Lucien - The protagonist, rescued from the Inquisition
- Simon (God has heard) - Lucien's father, who orchestrates the rescue
- Odette (wealthy) - Lucien's mother
- Guillaume (resolute protector) - Odette's wealthy cousin who assists in the rescue
- Estienne - Lucien's friend, also rescued
- Orielle - Estienne's sister, rescued with them

- Elie - Lucien's sister (mentioned briefly)
- Estienne and Orielle's mother (unnamed)

Central Themes

1. The Power of Familial Love and Sacrifice:

This theme is central to the chapter, demonstrated by the extraordinary lengths Simon and Odette go to in order to rescue Lucien. It's further reinforced by Guillaume's willingness to use his wealth and influence to help his relatives. The theme extends to Estienne and Orielle's family as well, highlighting how familial bonds can provide strength and support in times of crisis. The sacrifices made by the parents—from risking their own safety to accepting their children's dangerous path—underscore the depth of parental love.

2. The Conflict Between Faith and Safety:

The chapter explores the tension between holding true to one's religious convictions and ensuring personal and family safety. Lucien, Estienne, and Orielle's commitment to their Waldensian beliefs has put them in grave danger, forcing their families to confront the real-world consequences of their faith. The decision to send them to Switzerland represents a compromise between maintaining their beliefs and seeking safety, highlighting the difficult choices faced by religious minorities in times of persecution.

3. The Burden of Truth and Its Revelation:

Lucien's confession to his family about his involvement with the Waldensians is a pivotal moment in the chapter. It explores the weight of keeping significant truths from loved ones and the relief and consequences of finally revealing them. This theme touches on issues of trust within families, the desire to protect loved ones from difficult truths, and the importance of honesty in strengthening familial bonds, even in the face of danger.

Q&A

1. How do Lucien's parents learn about his arrest by the Inquisition?

A neighbor bursts into Simon's bakery with news from the town crier announcing Lucien's arrest.

2. Who helps Simon and Odette in their effort to rescue Lucien?

Odette's cousin, Guillaume, a wealthy merchant, uses his wealth and connections to help secure Lucien's release.

3. Besides Lucien, who else is rescued from the Inquisition's dungeons?

Estienne and his sister Orielle are also freed along with Lucien.

4. What plan is made for Lucien, Estienne, and Orielle's safety after their rescue?

They plan to seek refuge on Guillaume's farm in Switzerland, specifically in the region of Valais.

5. How does Simon support Lucien in his journey at the end of the chapter?

Simon gives Lucien a purse of coins to help him on his way and assures him that he will always have a home with his family.

Scripture Spotlight

1. Psalm 34:17-19 "When the righteous cry for help, the Lord hears and delivers them out of all their troubles. The Lord is near to the brokenhearted and saves the crushed in spirit. Many are the afflictions of the righteous, but the Lord delivers him out of them all."

This verse reflects the rescue of Lucien and his friends from their dire situation.

2. Jeremiah 29:11 "For I know the plans I have for you, declares the Lord, plans for welfare and not for evil, to give you a future and a hope."

This passage relates to the faith and trust the characters must have as they face an uncertain future.

3. 1 Corinthians 13:7 "Love bears all things, believes all things, hopes all things, endures all things."

This verse aligns with the theme of familial love and sacrifice demonstrated by the parents in their efforts to rescue and support their children.

Relevant Topics

1. Have you ever had to keep a significant secret from your family, and how did it affect your relationship with them?

Like Lucien, you might have faced situations where you felt you needed to hide important aspects of your life from your family. This could be about your beliefs, friendships, or personal struggles. Consider how keeping secrets impacts trust and communication in your family relationships. Reflect on the relief Lucien felt when he finally shared the truth, and think about the potential benefits of open communication with your loved ones.

2. How do you balance your desire for independence with your family's concern for your safety and well-being?

Like Lucien, Estienne, and Orielle preparing to leave for Switzerland, you might feel ready for more independence while your parents worry about your safety. Consider how you can demonstrate responsibility to earn your parents' trust. Think about ways to communicate your needs and aspirations clearly while also acknowledging your parents' concerns. How can you work together to find a balance between your growing autonomy and their protective instincts?

3. Is bribery justified in a situation like the one presented in this chapter? If not, why might the author have chosen to include it in this part of the story?

The use of bribery in this chapter raises complex moral questions. While bribing is generally considered unethical and illegal, the author may have included it to:

- *Highlight the desperate circumstances the characters face.*
- *Illustrate the moral complexities in a world where corruption is common.*
- *Show the lengths to which people might go to protect loved ones.*
- *Contrast different ethical standards between groups or individuals. Let's remember that Simon and Guillaume were not Waldensians.*
- *Create tension and advance the plot.*

It's important to note that the actions of characters don't necessarily reflect the author's moral stance or the overall message of the story. This scene could be meant to provoke thought about ethics in extreme situations.

When analyzing literature, it's crucial to consider the context, character motivations, and broader themes rather than assuming all character actions are meant to be models of behavior.

Activities

1. Organize a "Difficult Conversations" Workshop:

Set up a series of role-playing scenarios based on the challenging discussions in the chapter, such as Lucien revealing his involvement with the Waldensians to his parents. Practice having these conversations from different perspectives. Afterward, discuss strategies for approaching difficult topics with family members, focusing on active listening, empathy, and clear communication.

2. Develop a "Waldensian Rescue Network" Strategy:

Research contemporary situations where people face persecution for their beliefs. Create a plan for how you and your community could safely support and protect these individuals. Consider legal, ethical, and practical aspects of providing aid. Discuss the challenges and risks involved, and how this compares to historical examples like the Waldensians.

3. Create a "Family Bond" Time Capsule:

Inspired by the strong family connections in the chapter, assemble a time capsule that represents your relationship with your family. Include letters to your future self and family members, photos, and small objects that hold special meaning. Write about your current challenges, hopes, and the values that hold your family together. Set a date to open it in the future.

CHAPTER 19
The Inquisition's Fury

Summary

In this intense chapter, the Inquisition, led by the ruthless Inquisitor Talbot, launches a furious manhunt for the escaped Waldensians. The narrative alternates between the Inquisition's brutal tactics and the harrowing journey of Lucien, Estienne, and Orielle as they flee towards safety in Switzerland. The escapees face numerous challenges, including a terrifying wolf attack and the constant threat of capture. Meanwhile, Talbot punishes the guards responsible for the escape and intensifies his efforts, targeting Avignon and Lucien's family. The chapter vividly portrays the Inquisition's cruelty and the widespread fear it instills. After a perilous journey filled with narrow escapes and moments of despair, Lucien and his companions finally reach Valais, Switzerland, finding a moment of hope and freedom. The chapter ends with a stark contrast between their relief and the ongoing terror in Avignon as the Inquisition's campaign of fear continues unabated.

Key Characters

- Lucien - One of the main protagonists, fleeing from the Inquisition
- Estienne - Lucien's friend and fellow escapee
- Orielle - Estienne's sister, also fleeing with the group
- Guillaume - Helps the group escape and guides them part of the way
- Talbot (messenger of destruction) - The main antagonist and Inquisitor, leading the pursuit of the Waldensians
- Marlon (little hawk) - Talbot's trusted lieutenant
- Simon - Lucien's father
- Elie - Lucien's sister

Central Themes

1. Persecution and the Abuse of Power:

This theme is central to the chapter, embodied by the Inquisition's relentless pursuit of the Waldensians. Inquisitor Talbot's ruthless tactics, including the torture of guards and the terrorizing of Avignon's citizens, highlight the dangers of unchecked authority and religious extremism. The theme explores how power, when wielded without compassion or accountability, can lead to widespread suffering and injustice.

2. Resilience and Hope in the Face of Adversity:

Throughout their perilous journey, Lucien, Estienne, and Orielle demonstrate remarkable resilience. They face numerous challenges, including a wolf attack and the constant threat of capture, yet they persist. Their ability to find moments of hope and even triumph (such as successfully hunting the deer) amidst dire circumstances illustrates the human capacity for endurance and the power of hope in sustaining the spirit during difficult times.

3. The Price of Freedom and Faith:

The chapter vividly portrays the high cost of maintaining one's faith and pursuing freedom in the face of oppression. The escapees must leave behind their families, endure physical hardships, and live in constant fear. Meanwhile, those left behind in Avignon suffer under the Inquisition's regime of terror. This theme explores the sacrifices required to stay true to one's beliefs and the far-reaching consequences of standing up against tyranny.

Q&A

1. How does Inquisitor Talbot react to the news of the prisoners' escape?

Talbot reacts with intense fury, ordering a massive manhunt and punishing the guards responsible for the escape by sending them to the dungeons.

2. How does Guillaume assist the escapees?

Guillaume warns them of the approaching Inquisition, helps them escape from Grenoble, guides them part of the way to Annecy, and provides them with a letter of introduction before leaving them.

3. What unexpected danger do Lucien, Estienne, and Orielle face during their journey to Switzerland?

They face a terrifying wolf attack while camping in a clearing, forcing them to fight off the wolves and maintain vigilance throughout the night.

4. What strategy does Talbot employ to find the escaped Waldensians?

Talbot decides to target Avignon and Lucien's family, believing they are key to uncovering the Waldensian network.

5. How do Lucien and his companions obtain food during their journey?

At one point, Lucien successfully hunts a deer during his night watch, providing them with much-needed sustenance for their journey.

Scripture Spotlight

1. 2 Corinthians 4:8-9 "We are hard pressed on every side, but not crushed; perplexed, but not in despair; persecuted, but not abandoned; struck down, but not destroyed."

This verse mirrors the intense persecution and trials faced by Lucien, Estienne, Orielle, and their companions. They are constantly pursued by the

Inquisition, experiencing moments of despair and fear. However, despite being hard-pressed and persecuted, they remain resilient and undestroyed. Their escape from the Inquisition, the constant threats from wolves, and their arduous journey all reflect being "struck down, but not destroyed." The characters' perseverance, hope, and ultimate survival exemplify the message of enduring hardships without succumbing to them.

2. Isaiah 41:10 "So do not fear, for I am with you; do not be dismayed, for I am your God. I will strengthen you and help you; I will uphold you with my righteous right hand."

This verse captures the underlying faith and courage of the characters amidst their perilous journey. Despite the terror of being hunted by the Inquisition and the dangers they face along the way, such as the wolves and the physical exhaustion, they are encouraged to not fear. The belief that God is with them, offering strength and support, is a source of hope and comfort.

3. Proverbs 3:5-6 "Trust in the Lord with all your heart and lean not on your own understanding; in all your ways submit to him, and he will make your paths straight."

Throughout their escape, Lucien, Estienne, and Orielle must trust in something beyond their understanding to survive the dangers posed by the Inquisition and the wilderness. This verse encapsulates their reliance on faith over their own understanding and efforts. By submitting to a higher power and trusting in the Lord's guidance, they navigate the treacherous paths, finding refuge and ultimately reaching the safety of Valais. Their journey, filled with uncertainty and peril, aligns with the promise that submitting to divine guidance will lead them to safety.

Relevant Topics

1. How does the relentless pursuit of the Inquisition in the story compare to modern forms of persecution?

In the story, the Inquisition's relentless pursuit of Lucien and his companions symbolizes extreme persecution for one's beliefs. Today, people around the world still face persecution for their religious beliefs, political views, or other personal convictions. Modern persecution can take the form of discrimination, social ostracism, or even violence. By understanding historical examples, we can better recognize and stand against such injustices in our own time, advocating for tolerance and human rights.

2. How do the themes of trust and friendship in the story apply to your life today?

The themes of trust and friendship in the story show how vital it is to have a support system during tough times. Just as Lucien and his friends relied on each other, you too can lean on your friends and family when facing challenges. Trusting and supporting each other can make difficult journeys more manageable and help you feel less alone. Building strong, trusting relationships can provide you with the courage and strength to tackle whatever life throws your way.

3. How does the story highlight the importance of faith during difficult times, and how can this be relevant to your own experiences?

The story highlights the importance of faith as a source of strength and hope during difficult times. For Lucien and his companions, their faith provides them with the courage to keep going despite the dangers they face. In your own life, having faith—whether it's in a higher power, in yourself, or in the goodness of others—can help you navigate through tough situations. Faith can give you a sense of purpose, comfort, and resilience, helping you to face challenges with a positive outlook and determination.

Activities

1. Create a Survival Plan:

Imagine you are in Lucien's position, fleeing from the Inquisition. Plan a detailed escape route using modern tools. Mark safe houses, supply points, and potential threats on a map. Discuss with your group how you would stay hidden and what modern technology might help or hinder you.

2. Research Historical Persecution:

Research a historical period of persecution similar to the Inquisition, such as the Reformation and Counter-Reformation or the persecution of early Christians. Present your findings to the group, highlighting similarities and differences with the story. Discuss what lessons can be learned from these events.

3. Modern-Day Advocacy:

Identify a current issue of persecution or discrimination in the world today. Create an awareness campaign, including posters, social media posts, and a plan for a school or community event. Discuss how you can take action to support those who are persecuted and raise awareness among your peers.

CHAPTER 20
Safe Haven

Summary

In this chapter, Lucien, Estienne, and Orielle find refuge in a picturesque farmhouse in the Valais region of Switzerland. The narrative vividly describes their new sanctuary, emphasizing its beauty and the peace it offers after their harrowing journey. Welcomed by the kind-hearted housekeeper Henriette, they quickly settle into a new life that balances their mission of preserving forbidden texts with the daily demands of farm work. The chapter explores their adaptation to this new environment, detailing their farm chores and their continued dedication to transcribing and studying sacred texts. Throughout, there's a palpable sense of gratitude for their safety, tempered by concern for the loved ones they left behind. The friends find strength in their faith, their work, and their unity, viewing their efforts to preserve knowledge as a form of resistance against the persecution they fled. The chapter concludes with a moving prayer scene, underscoring their ongoing commitment to their beliefs and their hope for those still facing danger.

Key Characters

- Lucien - One of the main protagonists, adapting to farm life while continuing his scholarly work
- Estienne - Lucien's friend, sharing in the farm work and text preservation
- Orielle - Estienne's sister, also involved in farm life and scholarly pursuits
- Henriette (ruler of the home) - The housekeeper who welcomes and assists the trio in their new home

Central Themes

1. Sanctuary and Renewal:

This theme is central to the chapter, embodied in the farmhouse and its surroundings. The peaceful, beautiful setting offers a stark contrast to the persecution and danger the characters previously faced. It explores how a safe environment can facilitate physical, emotional, and spiritual healing. The theme also touches on the idea of starting anew and finding purpose in a different context.

2. Balance Between Intellectual and Physical Labor:

The chapter consistently highlights how the characters divide their time between copying forbidden texts and performing farm work. This theme explores the idea that both types of labor are valuable and complementary. It suggests that engaging in physical work can ground and supplement intellectual pursuits, providing a holistic approach to life and resistance.

3. Faith as a Source of Strength and Unity:

Throughout the chapter, the characters' faith serves as a unifying force and a source of comfort. Their religious convictions provide purpose to their work of preserving texts, offer solace when they worry about those left behind, and bind them together as a community. This theme explores how shared beliefs can provide resilience and meaning in the face of adversity and uncertainty.

Q&A

1. Where do Lucien, Estienne, and Orielle find refuge?

They find refuge in a farmhouse in the Valais region of Switzerland.

2. Who welcomes them to their new home?

Henriette, the housekeeper, welcomes them and provides them with food, blankets, and tea.

3. What two main types of work do the characters engage in at the farmhouse?

They split their time between farm work (such as milking cows, tending to sheep, gardening, and making cheese) and copying and studying forbidden religious texts.

4. How do the characters maintain connection with their families left behind?

They write carefully coded letters to their families, expressing their safety, love, and describing their new surroundings.

5. How does the chapter end?

The chapter ends with Lucien, Estienne, and Orielle praying together, asking for protection for their loved ones and reaffirming their commitment to their work and faith.

Scripture Spotlight

1. Colossians 3:23-24 "Whatever you do, work heartily, as for the Lord and not for men, knowing that from the Lord you will receive the inheritance as your reward. You are serving the Lord Christ."

This verse reflects the characters' dedication to both their farm work and their scholarly pursuits.

2. 1 Thessalonians 5:11 "Therefore encourage one another and build one another up, just as you are doing."

This verse reflects the support and unity among Lucien, Estienne, and Orielle as they adapt to their new life.

3. Matthew 5:16 "In the same way, let your light shine before others, so that they may see your good works and give glory to your Father who is in heaven."

This verse connects with the characters' view of their work preserving texts as a form of resistance and a way to spread truth.

Relevant Topics

1. Have you ever had to adapt to a new environment or culture? How does your experience compare to that of Lucien, Estienne, and Orielle?

Like the characters adjusting to farm life, you might have faced challenges adapting to a new school, neighborhood, or even country. Consider how you've balanced maintaining your identity with embracing new experiences and responsibilities.

2. In what ways do you balance intellectual pursuits with physical activities in your daily life?

The characters divide their time between studying texts and farm work. Reflect on how you manage your time between academic studies and physical activities or practical skills. How might this balance benefit your overall well-being and personal growth?

3. How do you stay connected with friends or family when physically separated from them?

The characters write coded letters to their families. In your digital age, you have many more options for staying in touch. Consider the pros and cons of various communication methods and how you can maintain meaningful connections despite distance.

Activities

1. Develop a "Balanced Life" Schedule:

Create a weekly schedule that balances intellectual pursuits with physical activities, mirroring the characters' lifestyle. Include time for studies, physical exercise, practical skills, and relaxation. Follow this schedule for a week and reflect on how it impacts your productivity and well-being.

2. Organize a "New Skills" Workshop:

Choose a practical skill mentioned in the chapter (like cheese-making, gardening, or animal care) and research how to do it. Prepare a short tutorial or demonstration for your friends or family. Reflect on the value of learning diverse skills and how they might be useful in various life situations.

3. Create a "Gratitude and Concern" Journal:

Start a journal where you daily write one thing you're grateful for and one concern you have for others, mirroring the characters' mix of appreciation for their safety and worry for those left behind. After a week, review your entries and reflect on how this practice affects your perspective on your life and the world around you.

CHAPTER 21
Orielle's Calling

Summary

In this emotionally charged chapter, Lucien and Estienne celebrate Orielle's birthday, marking a moment of joy in their new life. However, the peace is soon shattered when Lucien expresses his growing restlessness and desire to actively fight against the Inquisition. Their discussion is interrupted by the sudden arrival of their mother, Madeline, along with other refugees who bring devastating news. They recount a brutal attack by the Inquisition in the Valley of Pragelas, resulting in many deaths and disappearances, including Lucien's parents and sister. This news galvanizes the group, particularly Orielle, who realizes they can no longer remain in hiding. The chapter ends with a collective decision to actively resist the Inquisition, driven by their faith, determination, and newfound sense of purpose. Throughout, the narrative explores themes of family bonds, the cost of faith, and the transition from passive safety to active resistance.

Key Characters

- Orielle - The chapter's focal character, who experiences a significant shift in her resolve
- Lucien - Orielle's friend, who first expresses the need to actively fight the Inquisition
- Estienne - Orielle's brother, initially cautious but ultimately supportive of taking action
- Madeline - Orielle and Estienne's mother, who brings news of the Inquisition's attacks
- Henriette - The housekeeper who alerts them to the refugees' arrival

- Unnamed refugees - Including a man with silver hair and a woman whose son was taken, who provide firsthand accounts of the Inquisition's brutality
- Lucien's parents and sister - Mentioned as missing, presumed captured by the Inquisition

Central Themes

1. The Tension Between Safety and Duty:

This theme is central to the chapter, as the characters grapple with the conflict between their relative safety in their new home and their growing sense of responsibility to actively fight against the Inquisition. Lucien's restlessness and the group's ultimate decision to take action highlight the moral dilemma of choosing comfort over confronting injustice. This theme explores how personal security can sometimes conflict with larger ethical obligations.

2. The Power of Family and Community in Times of Crisis:

The chapter emphasizes the importance of familial and community bonds. From the celebration of Orielle's birthday to the emotional reunion with their mother, and the solidarity shown with the refugees, the narrative underscores how these relationships provide strength, support, and motivation in the face of adversity. This theme illustrates how shared experiences and mutual support can be crucial in overcoming challenges and making difficult decisions.

3. The Transformative Nature of Trauma and Loss:

The news of the Inquisition's brutal attack and the disappearance of loved ones serves as a catalyst for change in the characters, particularly Orielle. This theme explores how traumatic events can shift perspectives, ignite determination, and transform individuals from passive observers to active participants in resistance. It demonstrates how personal loss can fuel a broader commitment to justice and action.

Q&A

1. What special event occurs at the beginning of the chapter?

Lucien and Estienne surprise Orielle by celebrating her birthday, which is something they hadn't done before.

2. What concern does Lucien express about their current situation?

Lucien feels that they are hiding and not doing enough to help those suffering under the Inquisition. He wants to take more active measures against their enemies.

3. Who arrives unexpectedly at their refuge?

Madeline, Orielle and Estienne's mother, arrives with a group of refugees.

4. What devastating news do the refugees bring?

They bring news of a brutal attack by the Inquisition in the Valley of Pragelas, resulting in many deaths and disappearances, including Lucien's parents and sister.

5. How does Orielle's perspective change by the end of the chapter?

Orielle shifts from a more passive stance to a determination to actively resist the Inquisition, realizing that they can no longer remain in hiding.

Scripture Spotlight

1. Joshua 1:9 "Have I not commanded you? Be strong and courageous. Do not be frightened, and do not be dismayed, for the Lord your God is with you wherever you go."

This verse reflects the characters' resolve to face the challenges ahead.

2. Romans 12:15 "Rejoice with those who rejoice, weep with those who weep."

This verse aligns with the emotional range in the chapter, from celebrating Orielle's birthday to grieving for those lost to the Inquisition.

3. Proverbs 31:8-9 "Open your mouth for the mute, for the rights of all who are destitute. Open your mouth, judge righteously, defend the rights of the poor and needy."

This passage reflects the characters' decision to actively fight against the injustices of the Inquisition.

Relevant Topics

1. Have you ever felt torn between staying safe and standing up for what you believe in?

Like Lucien and the others, you might face situations where you need to choose between personal comfort and fighting for your beliefs. Consider how you balance safety with your sense of duty or justice in your own life.

2. How do you support friends or family members who are going through difficult times?

The characters in this chapter offer emotional support to each other and to the refugees. Think about how you can be there for your loved ones during their struggles, whether through active help or simply by listening.

3. How do you cope with unexpected bad news or sudden changes in your life?

The characters face devastating news about their loved ones. Reflect on your own coping mechanisms and support systems for dealing with difficult situations or sudden changes.

Activities

1. Create a "Surprise Celebration" Plan:

Design a surprise celebration for a friend or family member, inspired by Lucien and Estienne's gesture for Orielle. Plan the event, including a special meal, activities, and ways to make the person feel valued. Implement your plan and reflect on how small gestures can have a big impact on others' lives.

2. Develop a "Stand for Justice" Campaign:

Choose an issue in your school or community that you feel needs addressing. Create a plan to raise awareness and take action, similar to how the characters decide to resist the Inquisition. Design posters, write a speech, or organize a peaceful demonstration. Present your campaign to your peers and discuss how young people can make a difference.

3. Organize a "Family History" Interview Project:

Interview older family members about their experiences during significant historical events or personal challenges. Create a family history document or video compilation. Share your findings with your family and reflect on how past experiences shape current generations.

CHAPTER 22
A Desperate Search

Summary

In this chapter, Lucien and Estienne embark on a desperate search for Lucien's family in Avignon, despite the dangers posed by the Inquisition. They encounter old friends, Yves and Chapin, who warn them of an impending Inquisition assault. Undeterred, they continue their search, eventually meeting a young girl named Jeanne and her mother Clémentine, who provide crucial information about Lucien's family. They learn that Lucien's relatives were last seen with Guillaume, Lucien's mother's cousin, in the Valley of Pragelas. The chapter ends with Lucien and Estienne deciding to travel to Lyon, where they believe Guillaume might be found. Throughout, the narrative explores themes of loyalty, hope, and the risks of resistance against oppression. The chapter also highlights the widespread impact of the Inquisition's actions on Waldensian communities.

Key Characters

- Lucien - The protagonist, searching for his family
- Estienne - Lucien's friend and companion in the search
- Orielle - Mentioned at the beginning, she stays behind in Valais
- Yves - An old friend of Lucien who provides warnings about the Inquisition
- Chapin (shoemaker) - Yves' companion
- Jeanne (God is gracious) - A young girl who provides information about Lucien's family
- Clémentine (merciful and gentle) - Jeanne's mother, a Waldensian refugee
- Guillaume - Lucien's mother's cousin, last seen with Lucien's family (mentioned but not present)

Central Themes

1. Determination and Sacrifice:

The characters, especially Lucien and Estienne, display unwavering determination to find Lucien's family despite the immense dangers posed by the Inquisition. Their willingness to risk their lives highlights the theme of sacrifice, as they prioritize their loved ones and their mission over their personal safety.

2. Faith and Hope:

Throughout the chapter, the characters draw strength from their faith in God and their hope for a better future. Biblical references and prayers underscore their reliance on divine guidance and support. Despite the looming threat of the Inquisition, their faith provides a source of comfort and resilience.

3. Solidarity and Compassion:

The chapter emphasizes the importance of solidarity and compassion within the persecuted Waldensian community. Lucien and Estienne's interactions with Clémentine and Jeanne illustrate their commitment to helping others in need. The bond they form with fellow Waldensians reinforces the theme of unity in the face of oppression.

Q&A

1. Why does Orielle initially want to leave the safety of their refuge in the Valais?

Orielle wants to leave because she feels compelled to take action and help those suffering, particularly Lucien's family. She struggles with the idea of staying safe while knowing others are in danger.

2. How do Lucien and Estienne react to Orielle's desire to leave?

Lucien and Estienne are concerned for Orielle's safety and try to convince her to stay. They emphasize the dangers posed by the Inquisition and the importance of her contributions to their work in the Valais.

3. Who do Lucien and Estienne meet on their way to Avignon, and what crucial information do they provide?

They meet Yves and Chapin, who warn them that the Inquisition is aware of their presence and is planning an assault to capture the Mercier family. Yves also confirms that the Inquisition does not yet have Lucien's family in custody.

4. What motivates Lucien and Estienne to continue their search despite the dangers?

Their love for Lucien's family and their commitment to protecting them drive Lucien and Estienne to continue their search. They are determined to find Lucien's family before the Inquisition does, fueled by a sense of duty and hope.

5. What arrangement do Lucien and Estienne make with Clémentine and Jeanne, and why is it significant?

Lucien and Estienne promise to return for Clémentine and Jeanne after finding Lucien's family, showing their commitment to helping fellow Waldensians. This arrangement underscores the themes of solidarity and compassion within their community, as they ensure that no one is left behind.

Scripture Spotlight

1. Philippians 4:13 "I can do all things through him who strengthens me."

Lucien and Estienne draw strength from their faith in God, knowing that with His help, they can persevere through challenges and obstacles.

2. James 1:2-3 "Count it all joy, my brothers, when you meet trials of various kinds, for you know that the testing of your faith produces steadfastness."

This verse reflects the perspective of enduring trials with faith, understanding that hardships can strengthen one's resolve and faith in God's plan.

3. 1 Peter 5:7 "Casting all your anxieties on him, because he cares for you."

Lucien and Estienne find solace in entrusting their worries and fears to God, knowing that He cares deeply for them and their mission.

Relevant Topics

1. The characters in the story show resilience in the face of adversity. How can you build resilience in your own life?

Building resilience involves staying positive, adapting to change, and seeking support from friends, family, and faith communities. Learning from setbacks and staying determined helps you bounce back stronger.

2. What can you learn from Lucien and Estienne's journey about the importance of teamwork and friendship?

Their journey shows that teamwork and friendship are essential for overcoming challenges. Surrounding yourself with supportive friends and working together can make even daunting tasks more manageable.

3. Lucien and Estienne encounter fear and uncertainty. How can you manage your fears and find courage during tough times?

Facing fears starts with acknowledging them. Lean on your faith, talk to trusted adults or friends, and focus on positive actions you can take. Remember, God is with you through every challenge.

Activities

1. Create a Timeline:

Create a timeline of events from the chapter, highlighting key moments such as decisions made, risks faced, and alliances formed. Include illustrations or symbols to represent the emotions and challenges faced.

2. Role-Play and Debate:

Divide into groups and role-play scenarios where tough decisions must be made under pressure, similar to Lucien and Estienne's choices. Debate the ethical implications of their actions and discuss alternative solutions.

3. Artistic Expression:

Create artwork that symbolizes the themes of courage, resilience, and faith depicted in the chapter. Use various mediums such as painting, collage, or digital art to convey emotions and messages.

CHAPTER 23
The Black Death

Summary

In this chapter, Lucien and Estienne arrive in Lyon to find the city ravaged by the Black Death. The once-bustling metropolis is now a place of fear and despair, with makeshift hospitals and burning pyres dotting the landscape. As they search for Guillaume and Lucien's family, they discover that Guillaume has been using his resources to help the plague victims. After a tense search, they finally locate Guillaume working in a makeshift hospital. He confirms that Lucien's family is safe and hidden from the Inquisition. Guillaume then reveals that while working with the church and government on relief efforts, he has gained insider knowledge about their plans and weaknesses. The chapter ends with Guillaume explaining how the Inquisition is using the plague to further persecute the Waldensians and other perceived heretics, exploiting people's fear and desperation. The protagonists resolve to find a way to combat this injustice and spread hope in the face of overwhelming despair.

Key Characters

- Lucien - The protagonist searching for his family
- Estienne - Lucien's loyal friend and companion
- Guillaume - Lucien's mother's cousin, who has been helping plague victims and hiding Lucien's family
- Unnamed woman - Traveler who first informs Lucien and Estienne about the plague in Lyon
- Flagellants - Mentioned as an example of the religious fervor gripping the city
- The Inquisition - Not personified, but a significant presence influencing events

Central Themes

1. The Impact of Widespread Disease on Society:

This theme is central to the chapter, as the Black Death has transformed Lyon into a city of fear and despair. The plague's effects go beyond physical illness, reshaping social structures, religious practices, and power dynamics. The chapter explores how a pandemic can expose societal vulnerabilities and exacerbate existing tensions, leading to scapegoating and increased persecution of marginalized groups.

2. Compassion and Sacrifice in Times of Crisis:

Guillaume's actions embody this theme, as he risks his own safety to help plague victims and protect Lucien's family. This theme highlights how individuals can choose to respond to widespread suffering with empathy and self-sacrifice, even in the face of personal danger. It contrasts sharply with the opportunistic actions of the Inquisition and underscores the power of individual kindness in dark times.

3. The Manipulation of Fear for Political and Religious Control:

The chapter delves into how the Inquisition exploits the fear and uncertainty caused by the plague to tighten its grip on power. This theme explores the dangerous intersection of crisis, fear, and authoritarianism, showing how institutions can use people's desperation and need for explanation to further their own agendas and suppress dissent. It raises questions about the relationship between faith, power, and social control in times of widespread suffering.

Q&A

1. What unexpected situation do Lucien and Estienne encounter when they arrive in Lyon?

They find the city ravaged by the Black Death, with widespread fear, despair, and death.

2. How has Guillaume been spending his time in Lyon during the plague?

Guillaume has been using his resources to help plague victims, working in makeshift hospitals and providing food, water, and medicine.

3. What important information does Guillaume share with Lucien about his family?

Guillaume confirms that Lucien's family is safe and hidden where the Inquisition cannot find them.

4. What unexpected advantage has Guillaume gained through his relief work?

By working closely with the church and government on relief efforts, Guillaume has gained insider knowledge about their plans and weaknesses.

5. How is the Inquisition using the plague to their advantage, according to Guillaume?

The Inquisition is exploiting people's fear and desperation, using the plague as a tool to tighten their grip on power and persecute groups they deem heretical, such as the Waldensians.

Scripture Spotlight

1. Matthew 25:35-36 "For I was hungry and you gave me food, I was thirsty and you gave me drink, I was a stranger and you welcomed me, I was naked and you clothed me, I was sick and you visited me, I was in prison and you came to me."

This verse reflects Guillaume's actions in helping the plague victims.

2. Psalm 91:5-6 "You will not fear the terror of the night, nor the arrow that flies by day, nor the pestilence that stalks in darkness, nor the destruction that wastes at noonday."

This passage relates to the fear and devastation caused by the plague.

3. Proverbs 3:27 "Do not withhold good from those to whom it is due, when it is in your power to do it."

This verse aligns with Guillaume's decision to use his resources to help others.

Relevant Topics

1. How does the reaction to the plague in Lyon compare to modern responses to pandemics?

Like in Lyon, you've likely seen how a widespread disease can cause fear and changes in society. Consider how COVID-19 affected your community. Did you notice changes in behavior, increased fear, or attempts to find someone to blame?

2. Have you witnessed acts of compassion during difficult times, similar to Guillaume's actions?

Think about recent crises in your community. Did you see people stepping up to help others, even at personal risk? Reflect on how individual acts of kindness can make a difference in challenging times.

3. How does the chapter's exploration of the relationship between fear, faith, and power relate to current events?

The chapter shows how fear can be exploited by those in power. In today's world, how do you see fear influencing political or social dynamics? How can faith or personal convictions provide strength in facing such challenges?

Activities

1. Create a "Pandemic Response" Plan:

Design a comprehensive plan to address a hypothetical pandemic in your community. Include strategies for healthcare, resource distribution, and public communication. Consider how to prevent panic and misinformation. Present your plan to classmates or family members and discuss its strengths and potential challenges.

2. Organize a "Hidden Heroes" Research Project:

Research individuals in your community who have made significant contributions during times of crisis, similar to Guillaume. Interview them if possible. Create a presentation or social media campaign to highlight their efforts. Reflect on how ordinary people can make extraordinary impacts.

3. Host a "Compassion in Action" Challenge:

Organize a week-long challenge in your school or community where participants perform daily acts of kindness. Keep a journal of your actions and their impacts. At the end of the week, host a discussion about the experience and how small acts can create positive change.

CHAPTER 24
The Waldensian's Stand

Summary

In this climactic chapter, Lucien and Estienne join the Waldensian resistance in the Valley of Prali after learning of the Pope's decree for their extermination. They reunite with Lucien's family and the Sage, who miraculously escaped from the Inquisition. The Waldensians prepare for battle, crafting weapons and fortifying their position. Despite initial disappointment when expected allies fail to arrive, they remain resolute. The chapter culminates in a fierce battle against the Church's forces. Lucien initiates the conflict by shooting the enemy commander, and the Waldensians fight bravely. Just as they begin to falter, reinforcements from the Cottian Alps arrive, turning the tide of battle. The Waldensians emerge victorious, securing their freedom and faith.

Key Characters

- Lucien - The protagonist, leading the Waldensian resistance
- Estienne - Lucien's loyal friend and fellow fighter
- The Sage - A respected leader who escapes the Inquisition and inspires the Waldensians
- Odette - Lucien's mother
- Simon - Lucien's father
- Elie - Lucien's younger sister
- Guillaume - Mentioned as the one who informed them about the Pope's decree
- Unnamed Church commander - The leader of the attacking forces, killed by Lucien's arrow

Central Themes

1. Faith and Resilience in the Face of Adversity:

This theme is central to the chapter, as the Waldensians face overwhelming odds yet remain steadfast in their beliefs. The Sage's miraculous escape, the group's preparation for battle, and their unwavering resolve despite initial setbacks all exemplify this theme. It explores how faith can provide strength and unity in times of extreme hardship, enabling people to persevere against seemingly insurmountable challenges.

2. The Power of Community and Unity:

The chapter strongly emphasizes the importance of community solidarity. From the emotional reunions to the collective effort in preparing for battle, and finally in the unified stand against the enemy, the Waldensians demonstrate the strength that comes from a tightly-knit community. This theme highlights how shared beliefs and common purpose can create a formidable force, even when facing a much larger and better-equipped opponent.

3. Sacrifice and Commitment to Ideals:

Throughout the chapter, characters are willing to risk everything for their beliefs and freedom. Lucien and Estienne's decision to join the resistance, leaving their families behind, and the entire community's readiness to fight to the death rather than surrender their faith, illustrate this theme. It explores the idea that some principles are worth fighting and potentially dying for, examining the lengths people will go to defend their ideals and way of life.

Q&A

1. What major event prompts Lucien and Estienne to join the Waldensian resistance in Prali?

They learn of the Pope's decree calling for the complete extermination of the Waldensians.

2. How does the Sage's return impact the Waldensians?

The Sage's miraculous escape from the Inquisition and his return greatly boost morale, providing inspiration and leadership to the Waldensian community.

3. What unexpected challenge do the Waldensians face before the battle?

Their expected allies from the Cottian Alps initially refuse to come to their aid, citing the journey as too treacherous and risky.

4. How does Lucien initiate the battle against the Church forces?

Lucien shoots an arrow that kills the Church commander after refusing the call to surrender.

5. What turns the tide of the battle in favor of the Waldensians?

The unexpected arrival of reinforcements from the Cottian Alps, who attack the Church forces from the flank, leading to a decisive victory for the Waldensians.

Scripture Spotlight

1. Psalm 46:1-3 "God is our refuge and strength, a very present help in trouble. Therefore we will not fear though the earth gives way, though the mountains be moved into the heart of the sea, though its waters roar and foam, though the mountains tremble at its swelling."

This verse reflects the Waldensians' steadfast faith in the face of overwhelming odds.

2. Ephesians 6:13 "Therefore take up the whole armor of God, that you may be able to withstand in the evil day, and having done all, to stand firm."

This passage relates to the Waldensians' preparation for battle and their determination to stand firm in their faith.

3. Psalm 18:39 "For you equipped me with strength for the battle; you made those who rise against me sink under me."

This verse corresponds to the Waldensians' unexpected victory in battle.

4. Hebrews 11:1 "Now faith is the assurance of things hoped for, the conviction of things not seen."

This verse reflects the Waldensians' unwavering faith, even when their situation seemed hopeless.

Biblical Parallels

The Sage's providential escape from the clutches of the Inquisition shares several parallels with the biblical story found in Acts 12:6-11, where Peter is miraculously freed from prison by an angel of the Lord. Here are some similarities:

1. **Miraculous Escape from Imprisonment:**
   - Peter is in prison, guarded by soldiers and bound with chains. An angel appears, his chains fall off, and the angel leads him past the guards and out of the prison, miraculously opening the iron gate to the city.
   - The Sage is held in a dungeon by the Inquisition, facing torture and the threat of death. He experiences a miraculous escape when his

cell door opens and the guards are put into a deep sleep, allowing him to flee.

2. **Divine Intervention:**
   - The intervention of an angel, a divine messenger, emphasizes that Peter's escape is orchestrated by God.
   - The Sage attributes his escape to divine providence, feeling that God guided him and provided the means for his escape, similar to Peter's experience of divine assistance.

3. **Unexpected Freedom Leading to Reunification:**
   - After escaping, Peter goes to the house of Mary, where many are gathered in prayer. They are astonished and overjoyed to see him, having feared the worst.
   - The Sage returns to his community, who are overwhelmed with joy and disbelief at seeing him alive, mirroring the surprise and elation of Peter's community.

4. **Strengthening of Faith:**
   - Peter's miraculous escape strengthens the faith of the early Christians, affirming God's power and presence.
   - The Sage's escape reinforces the faith of the Waldensians, serving as a testament to the power of faith and divine intervention, encouraging them to persevere.

5. **Symbol of Divine Protection:**
   - Peter's deliverance serves as a powerful symbol of God's protection over His followers, inspiring continued faith and resilience among the early Christians.
   - The Sage's survival and return act as a powerful symbol of divine protection and guidance, motivating the Waldensians to remain steadfast in their faith despite persecution.

Both Peter's escape in the Bible and the Sage's fictional escape in the chapter show how faith in God can lead to amazing miracles. These stories remind us that even in the toughest times, believing in something greater can bring unexpected help and give us hope when things seem darkest.

Relevant Topics

1. In what ways can you prepare yourself to face unexpected challenges?

The Waldensians prepared for battle both physically and mentally. While you're unlikely to face actual combat, consider how you can develop resilience, problem-solving skills, and mental toughness to handle life's challenges.

2. How do you deal with disappointment when expected support doesn't come through?

The Waldensians initially didn't receive the help they expected from their allies. Reflect on how you handle situations where you don't get the support you anticipated. How can you remain resilient and find alternative solutions?

3. How do you reconcile peaceful beliefs with the need to sometimes take strong action?

The Waldensians, despite their peaceful faith, had to fight to defend themselves. In your life, how do you balance non-violent principles with the need to actively oppose injustice or defend your rights?

Activities

1. Create a "Community Strength" Mural:

Design and paint a mural that represents the strength of your community. Include symbols of unity, resilience, and shared values. Display your mural in a public space and explain its meaning to others. Reflect on how art can inspire and unite people during challenging times.

2. Organize a "Historical Reenactment" Role-play:

Set up a role-playing scenario based on the Waldensians' preparations for battle. Assign roles such as leaders, craftsmen, and defenders. Create challenges that require teamwork and problem-solving. After the activity, discuss how historical events can teach us about cooperation and resilience in modern contexts.

3. Develop a "Stand for Your Beliefs" Debate:

Choose a current controversial topic. Research both sides of the issue and organize a structured debate. Argue your position respectfully, using facts and logical reasoning. Afterward, reflect on the importance of understanding different perspectives and standing up for your beliefs in a constructive manner.

CHAPTER 25
The Enduring Flame

Summary

This last chapter in the book takes place in the aftermath of the
Waldensians' victory against the Church forces. It opens with Lucien and
Estienne surveying the battlefield, reflecting on the cost of their victory. The
Sage then leads a funeral service for the fallen, drawing on Scripture to offer
hope and comfort to the grieving Waldensians. He specifically honors fallen
heroes Benoit, Lazare, and Remy, emphasizing their courage and faith. The
Sage then recounts the recent battle, praising God for their victory and
highlighting the crucial arrival of reinforcements from the Cottian Alps. The
chapter concludes with a private conversation between Lucien and Estienne,
where Lucien confesses his feelings for Orielle and decides to go find her.

Key Characters

- Lucien - The protagonist, reflecting on the battle and deciding to find
  Orielle
- Estienne - Lucien's close friend and confidant
- The Sage - The spiritual leader of the Waldensians who delivers the
  funeral service and victory speech
- Benoit - A fallen hero mentioned in the memorial
- Lazare - Another fallen hero remembered in the service
- Remy - The third fallen hero honored by the Sage
- Orielle - The object of Lucien's affections, not present but
  significantly mentioned

Central Themes

1. The Tension Between Victory and Loss:

This theme is central to the chapter, as the Waldensians grapple with the aftermath of their battle. While they have achieved a significant victory against overwhelming odds, they are also faced with the stark reality of the lives lost in the process. The chapter explores how communities navigate the complex emotions of triumph and grief, celebrating their survival while mourning their fallen comrades.

2. Faith as a Source of Hope and Resilience:

Throughout the chapter, faith plays a crucial role in providing comfort and strength to the Waldensians. The Sage's funeral service, heavily rooted in Scripture, offers hope of resurrection and reunion with the deceased. This theme illustrates how religious belief can provide solace and purpose in the face of tragedy and uncertainty.

3. The Power of Community and Unity:

The chapter emphasizes the importance of communal bonds in overcoming adversity. From the shared grief and hope during the funeral service to the recounting of how the Cottian Alps reinforcements turned the tide of battle, the narrative underscores how unity and mutual support are vital to the Waldensians' survival and success. This theme extends to personal relationships as well, as seen in Estienne's supportive response to Lucien's confession about Orielle.

Q&A

1. What event does the Sage lead at the beginning of the chapter?

The Sage leads a funeral service for the fallen Waldensians.

2. Which three fallen heroes does the Sage specifically mention and honor?

The Sage honors Benoit, Lazare, and Remy.

3. What crucial event does the Sage highlight as turning the tide of the battle?

The Sage emphasizes the arrival of reinforcements from the Cottian Alps as the turning point in the battle.

4. What Scripture does the Sage use to comfort the Waldensians about their fallen comrades?

The Sage quotes from 1 Thessalonians 4:16-17, which speaks about the resurrection of the dead and reunion with Christ.

5. What personal confession does Lucien make to Estienne at the end of the chapter?

Lucien confesses that he misses Orielle and decides to go find her.

Scripture Spotlight

1. 1 Thessalonians 4:16-17 "For the Lord himself will descend from heaven with a cry of command, with the voice of an archangel, and with the sound of the trumpet of God. And the dead in Christ will rise first. Then we who are alive, who are left, will be caught up together with them in the clouds to meet the Lord in the air, and so we will always be with the Lord."

This verse is directly quoted by the Sage during the funeral service. It offers hope to the Waldensians by promising a future resurrection and reunion with their fallen comrades.

2. Isaiah 40:31 "But they who wait for the Lord shall renew their strength; they shall mount up with wings like eagles; they shall run and not be weary; they shall walk and not faint."

This passage relates to the renewed strength and hope the Waldensians find after their victory and through the Sage's words, despite their exhaustion and grief.

3. Revelation 21:4 "He will wipe away every tear from their eyes, and death shall be no more, neither shall there be mourning, nor crying, nor pain anymore, for the former things have passed away."

This verse aligns with the hope offered in the funeral service—a future where all sorrow and death will be eliminated, providing comfort to those mourning their losses.

Relevant Topics

1. How do you cope with mixed emotions after achieving a goal that came at a high cost?

Like the Waldensians celebrating victory while mourning losses, you might face situations where success is bittersweet. Reflect on how you can honor sacrifices made while still acknowledging achievements.

2. In what ways can shared beliefs or values unite people during difficult times?

The Waldensians found strength in their shared faith. Consider how common causes or beliefs in your community can bring people together during challenges, such as during a pandemic or after a natural disaster.

3. How do you balance honoring those who have passed while moving forward with your own life?

The Waldensians memorialized their fallen while preparing for the future. Think about how you can remember and respect those you've lost while continuing to pursue your own goals and dreams.

Activities

1. Create a "Memorial Wall":

Design a digital or physical memorial wall honoring people who have made significant sacrifices for a cause you believe in. Research and include brief biographies, quotes, and images. Present your wall to classmates or family, explaining the impact of these individuals and how their legacy relates to current issues.

2. Host a "Courageous Conversations" Workshop:

Organize a workshop teaching peers how to have difficult but necessary conversations, like Lucien confessing his feelings to Estienne. Create role-playing scenarios and teach communication techniques. Discuss the importance of trust and support in friendships.

3. Design a "Future Hope" Art Installation:

Create an art piece or installation representing hope for the future, inspired by the Sage's message of resurrection. Use any medium (digital art, sculpture, painting, etc.). Display your work and invite viewers to add their own symbols or messages of hope. Reflect on how art can express complex emotions and inspire others during challenging times.

APPENDIX 1
Historical Facts About the Medieval Times

Imagine living in a time where the landscape of society was as rigid as the stone castles dotting the countryside. Welcome to the Medieval Times, an era spanning from the 5th to the late 15th century, where life revolved around the feudal system. Kings and lords held the power, granting land to vassals in exchange for military service and loyalty. The peasants, or serfs, worked the land and produced food, receiving protection from their lords in return. This structured hierarchy was the bedrock of medieval society, dictating the roles and relationships of everyone within it.

In the midst of this feudal world, monumental events were shaping the future of Europe. The Crusades, a series of religious wars sanctioned by the Catholic Church, aimed to reclaim Jerusalem and other holy sites from Muslim control. Beginning in 1096 and continuing for centuries, these crusades were not just battles for land but also for religious supremacy, leaving lasting impacts on trade, cultural exchange, and even the strained relations between Christians and Muslims.

The 14th century brought a catastrophe that would leave an indelible mark on history: the Black Death. This devastating pandemic, caused by the Bubonic Plague, swept through Europe between 1347 and 1352, wiping out nearly one-third of the population. The aftermath was profound, leading to labor shortages, shifts in the feudal system, and changing attitudes towards the Church and mortality. Entire villages were abandoned, and the social fabric of Europe was irrevocably altered.

Amidst the turmoil, a beacon of legal reform emerged in 1215 with the signing of the Magna Carta by King John of England. This document was revolutionary, limiting the power of the monarchy and establishing principles such as the right to a fair trial and protection from arbitrary imprisonment. It laid the groundwork for modern democracy and the rule of law, echoing through the centuries as a symbol of justice and liberty.

During these times of conflict and change, the arts and architecture flourished, giving rise to the awe-inspiring Gothic cathedrals. Characterized by pointed arches, ribbed vaults, and flying buttresses, these structures reached new heights, both literally and figuratively. Notre-Dame in Paris and Chartres Cathedral are prime examples, their towering spires and intricate stained glass windows drawing the faithful and the curious alike, symbolizing the aspirations of a society reaching towards the heavens.

Education also took root in this fertile ground of change. The first universities, such as those in Bologna, Paris, and Oxford, became centers of learning and scholarship. Here, students studied the liberal arts, theology, and law, all taught in Latin. These institutions preserved and advanced knowledge, ensuring that the intellectual heritage of the ancient world was not lost to the ravages of time.

Yet, the Medieval Times were not without their darker aspects. The Hundred Years' War between England and France raged from 1337 to 1453, marked by battles like Agincourt and the heroism of Joan of Arc. This conflict fostered national identities and contributed to the eventual decline of feudalism.

Simultaneously, the Inquisition cast a shadow over Europe. Established by the Catholic Church to combat heresy, it became infamous for its use of torture and execution to maintain religious orthodoxy. This period of persecution left a scar on the collective consciousness of the continent, influencing religious and social life profoundly.

Even in these turbulent times, the spirit of exploration and conquest was alive. The Viking Age, from around 793 to 1066, saw Norse explorers and raiders venturing far from their Scandinavian homelands. They sailed to the British Isles, mainland Europe, and even as far as North America, establishing settlements and leaving a lasting legacy in places like Iceland, Greenland, and Normandy.

Through it all, monastic life provided a counterpoint to the era's violence and upheaval. Monasteries were havens of learning, agriculture, and charity. Monks and nuns, devoted to religious service, prayer, and the preservation of manuscripts, played a crucial role in maintaining knowledge and culture.

In the tapestry of Medieval Times, each thread of history weaves a story of resilience, conflict, innovation, and faith, creating a rich and complex picture of an era that shaped the world we live in today.

Average Life Span and Marriage Age

During the Medieval period, life expectancy was significantly lower than in modern times. The average life span for peasants was around 33 years, while nobility could expect to live into their 40s. High infant mortality rates, disease, and lack of medical knowledge all contributed to this shorter life expectancy.

Marriage practices varied across social classes and regions. For peasants and lower classes, the average age of marriage was typically in the late teens to early twenties. Women often married between 16 and 20 years old, while men usually married in their early to mid-20s.

For nobility and royalty, marriages were often arranged for political or economic reasons, and could occur at much younger ages. It wasn't uncommon for noble girls to be betrothed as young as 12 and married by 14, although consummation might be delayed until they were older. Noble boys might be betrothed young but typically didn't marry until their late teens or early 20s.

It's important to note that these early marriages didn't necessarily mean early parenthood. Many couples, especially among the nobility, delayed having children until they were older and more financially stable.

These marriage practices and life expectancies were influenced by factors such as high mortality rates, economic necessities, and social customs of the time.

APPENDIX 2
Historical Facts About the Catholic Church

Imagine a world where the towering spires of cathedrals pierced the sky, and the sound of church bells echoed across towns and villages. This was the world of medieval Europe, where the Catholic Church stood as a dominant force, guiding the spiritual and often the temporal lives of its people. The Catholic Church wielded immense influence, shaping the course of history through its doctrines, institutions, and leaders.

The formation of the Catholic Church was a complex process that unfolded over several centuries after the life of Jesus Christ. It began with the establishment of a basic structure based on apostolic succession, with bishops seen as the successors to the apostles. As the Church grew, it faced theological disputes, leading to ecumenical councils like the First Council of Nicaea in 325 CE, which established core Catholic beliefs through creeds. A pivotal moment came with Emperor Constantine's conversion and the Edict of Milan in 313 CE, which legalized Christianity and allowed for public worship.

This period saw the rise of influential Church Fathers who developed Catholic doctrine and addressed heresies. Gradually, the Bishop of Rome asserted primacy over other bishops, centralizing authority. Throughout the Middle Ages, the Church expanded its hierarchical structure and influence across Europe, with monasticism playing a crucial role in preserving knowledge and spreading the faith. The Church also faced significant challenges, including the Great Schism of 1054 and internal corruption, leading to various reform movements. These developments collectively transformed the early Catholic movement into the structured and influential institution known as the Catholic Church.

In the early Middle Ages, the Catholic Church provided stability in a time of chaos following the fall of the Roman Empire. As kingdoms and empires rose and fell, the Church remained a constant, preserving knowledge and fostering a sense of unity among disparate peoples. Monasteries, in particular, became beacons of learning and culture. Monks, dedicated to a life of prayer and work, painstakingly copied ancient texts, ensuring the survival of classical knowledge and laying the groundwork for future intellectual revival.

The papacy emerged as a powerful institution during this period. One of the most notable popes was Gregory the Great, who served from 590 to 604. Gregory's reforms in liturgy and administration solidified the Church's spiritual authority and its role in governing the Christian world. His contributions to the development of Gregorian Chant also left a lasting legacy on Western liturgical music.

As the Middle Ages progressed, the Church's influence extended beyond spiritual matters into the realm of politics. The Investiture Controversy, which erupted in the 11th century, exemplified this struggle for power between the papacy and secular rulers. Pope Gregory VII and Emperor Henry IV clashed over the appointment of bishops, a conflict that highlighted the Church's desire to assert its independence and authority over secular matters. This dispute eventually led to the Concordat of Worms in 1122, which established a compromise between the two powers.

One of the most significant events in Church history was the launch of the Crusades. Beginning in 1096, these religious wars aimed to reclaim Jerusalem and other holy sites from Muslim control. Pope Urban II's call to arms at the Council of Clermont inspired thousands to take up the cross. The Crusades not only altered the political landscape of the Middle East but also had profound economic and cultural impacts on Europe, fostering trade and the exchange of ideas between different cultures.

The 13th century saw the rise of two influential mendicant orders: the Franciscans and the Dominicans. Founded by St. Francis of Assisi and St. Dominic respectively, these orders emphasized poverty, preaching, and a return to the simplicity of the early Church. Their members traveled extensively, ministering to the poor and spreading the Christian message. The Franciscans, in particular, became known for their care for the environment and animals, reflecting St. Francis's love for all creation.

In 1215, the Fourth Lateran Council convened under Pope Innocent III. This council was a turning point in Church history, as it addressed issues of heresy, clerical reform, and the administration of sacraments. One of its most enduring decrees was the establishment of the doctrine of transubstantiation, affirming the belief that the bread and wine of the Eucharist become the actual body and blood of Christ.

The period of the Avignon Papacy from 1309 to 1377, when the popes resided in Avignon, France, rather than Rome, marked a turbulent chapter for the Church. This era, often referred to as the "Babylonian Captivity of the Church," saw the papacy heavily influenced by French kings, leading to widespread criticism and calls for reform. The return to Rome and the subsequent Western Schism, where multiple claimants to the papal throne emerged, further eroded the Church's authority and unity.

Throughout these centuries, the Church also faced internal challenges and calls for reform. Figures like St. Catherine of Siena and John Wycliffe emerged, criticizing corruption and advocating for a return to spiritual purity. Wycliffe's translation of the Bible into English laid the groundwork for later reformers and highlighted the growing desire for access to scripture in the vernacular.

As the Middle Ages drew to a close, the Catholic Church stood at a crossroads, its foundations shaken by internal and external pressures. The dawn of the Renaissance and the Reformation would bring profound changes, but the medieval Church's legacy of scholarship, art, and spiritual guidance continued to influence the course of Western civilization. Its towering cathedrals, philosophical treatises, and enduring rituals remained as testaments to an era where faith and power were inextricably linked, shaping the destiny of millions.

Catholic Church's Pagan Traditions

During the Middle Ages, the Catholic Church incorporated various pagan traditions into its practices and doctrines, often as a means of facilitating the conversion of non-Christian populations. This process, known as syncretism, allowed the Church to expand its influence while making Christianity more familiar and accessible to new converts. Here's an overview of how this occurred:

1. **Absorption of local deities**: Many pagan gods and goddesses were recast as Christian saints, allowing new converts to continue venerating familiar figures within a Christian context.
2. **Adaptation of festivals**: Pagan seasonal celebrations were often repurposed as Christian holidays. For example, the winter solstice festivities became associated with Christmas, and spring fertility rituals were linked to Easter.
3. **Sacred sites**: Pagan temples and sacred groves were frequently converted into Christian churches or shrines, maintaining the spiritual significance of these locations for local populations.
4. **Symbolic imagery**: Pagan symbols were often reinterpreted with Christian meanings. For instance, the Celtic cross incorporated the sun cross into Christian iconography.
5. **Ritual practices**: Some pagan rituals were adapted into Christian ceremonies, such as the use of candles, incense, and the veneration of relics.
6. **Concept of purgatory**: The idea of an intermediary state after death, where souls could be purified, drew from various pagan afterlife beliefs.

7. **Marian devotion**: The heightened veneration of the Virgin Mary in some ways paralleled the worship of mother goddesses in pagan traditions.

8. **Worship of saints**: The veneration of saints in some ways mirrored the polytheistic practices of paganism, with different saints associated with various aspects of life, similar to how pagan gods had specific domains.

9. **Holy water**: The use of consecrated water for blessings and purification has roots in pagan purification rituals.

10. **Rosary beads**: The practice of using prayer beads has parallels in various pagan traditions, including Hindu and Buddhist practices.

11. **Harvest festivals**: Many local harvest celebrations were incorporated into the Christian calendar, often associated with saints' days.

12. **Yule log**: The Christmas tradition of the Yule log originated from pagan winter solstice celebrations.

13. **Easter eggs and bunnies**: These symbols of fertility from pagan spring festivals were incorporated into Easter celebrations.

14. **All Saints' Day**: This holiday, celebrated on November 1, coincides with the Celtic festival of Samhain and incorporates elements of ancestor veneration common in many pagan traditions.

15. **Church gargoyles**: These decorative elements on Gothic churches often incorporated pagan nature spirits and protective deities.

16. **Pilgrimages**: The practice of traveling to holy sites has roots in pagan traditions of visiting sacred groves, springs, and mountains.

17. **Monasticism**: While distinctly Christian in its development, some aspects of monastic life, such as asceticism and contemplative practices, had parallels in pagan traditions.

This syncretism was not universally accepted within the Church, and it sometimes led to tensions and debates about orthodoxy. However, it played a significant role in the spread and acceptance of Christianity across Europe during the Middle Ages. It's important to note that while these practices were incorporated, the core theological doctrines of Christianity remained distinct from pagan beliefs. The Church sought to reinterpret and Christianize these elements rather than adopt pagan theology wholesale.

The Catholic Doctrine of Immortality

The Catholic doctrine of the immortality of the soul, while central to Church teachings, has roots that can be traced back to pagan philosophical traditions, particularly Greek philosophy. Here's an explanation of how this concept was influenced by and incorporated from pagan thought:

1. Platonic influence:

- The Greek philosopher Plato (428/427-348/347 BCE) was one of the earliest and most influential proponents of the soul's immortality.
- In his dialogues, particularly "Phaedo," Plato argued for the existence of an immortal, immaterial soul distinct from the body.

2. Aristotelian concepts:

- Aristotle, while disagreeing with Plato on many points, also contributed to the concept of the soul, though his views were more nuanced.
- His idea of the soul as the form or essence of a living being influenced later Catholic thinkers.

3. Neo-Platonism:

- This philosophical school, particularly through thinkers like Plotinus, further developed ideas about the soul's immortality and its relationship to the divine.
- Neo-Platonism had a significant impact on early Catholic theology.

4. Synthesis with Catholic thought:

- Early Church Fathers, particularly those with a Greek philosophical background, incorporated these ideas into Catholic theology.
- St. Augustine, heavily influenced by Neo-Platonism, played a crucial role in integrating the concept of an immortal soul into Catholic doctrine.

5. Contrast with early Hebrew thought:

- The early Hebrew concept of the soul (nephesh) was more holistic, referring to the whole person rather than an immortal, separable entity.
- The Greek philosophical concept of an immortal soul was gradually assimilated into Catholic thinking, diverging from earlier Hebraic and Christian views.

6. Gnostic influences:

- While the Church opposed Gnosticism, some Gnostic ideas about the soul's divine nature and its separation from the material world influenced Catholic thought.

7. Adaptation and reinterpretation:

- The Church adapted these pagan philosophical concepts, reinterpreting them within a Christian framework of creation, fall, and redemption.

8. Medieval scholasticism:

- Theologians like Thomas Aquinas further developed the doctrine, synthesizing Aristotelian philosophy with Catholic theology.

It's important to note that while the concept of an immortal soul became central to Catholic doctrine, it has been a subject of theological debate and interpretation throughout Church history. The incorporation of this pagan philosophical concept into Catholic theology exemplifies how the Church often assimilated and reinterpreted pre-existing ideas within its theological framework.

Sunday Worship

The Catholic practice of Sunday worship, while primarily based on later Christian tradition, does have some origins and influences from pagan practices. Here's an explanation of how this came about:

1. Early Christian practice:

- Jesus and early Christians observed Sabbath on Saturday.
- As Christianity spread to Gentile communities, the emphasis on Sunday worship increased.
- By the 3rd century AD Sunday worship became more established, though some Christian communities still observed both Saturday and Sunday.
- Tertullian (c. 155-220 AD) defended Sunday observance against those who accused Christians of sun worship.

2. Roman influence:

- In the Roman calendar, Sunday was "dies Solis" (day of the Sun), dedicated to the sun god.
- This aligned with the Christian symbolism of Christ as the "Light of the World."

3. Constantine's decree:

- In 321 CE, Roman Emperor Constantine issued a decree making Sunday a day of rest for all citizens, not just Christians.
- This decree was influenced by both Christian practice and the Roman veneration of the sun.

4. Mithraic influence:

- The cult of Mithras, popular among Roman soldiers, also held Sunday as sacred.
- This may have eased the transition for some pagans converting to Christianity.

5. Syncretism:

- As Christianity spread, incorporating Sunday worship made it easier for pagans to adapt to Christian practices.

6. Agricultural societies:

- Many pagan cultures already had traditions of rest days aligned with lunar or solar cycles.
- Sunday worship could be seen as a continuation of these practices.

7. Biblical reinterpretation:

- The Church reinterpreted the Sabbath commandment to apply to Sunday, viewing it as the fulfillment of the Old Testament Sabbath.

8. Gradual development:

- The shift from Saturday to Sunday worship was gradual and not uniform across all early Christian communities.

9. Council of Laodicea:

- In 364 CE, this council discouraged Christians from "Judaizing" by resting on Saturday, further cementing Sunday as the Christian day of worship.

10. Theological justification:

- The Church developed theological reasons for Sunday worship, emphasizing it as a celebration of the new creation in Christ and observance of the Lord's Day.

It's important to note that while there were pagan influences, the primary reason for Christian Sunday worship was theological—the commemoration of Christ's resurrection. The adoption of Sunday also served to differentiate Christianity from Judaism. The pagan elements were more about easing the transition for converts and aligning with existing social structures rather than adopting pagan theology.

APPENDIX 3
Historical Facts About the Inquisition

In the annals of medieval history, the Inquisition stands as a stark reminder of religious fervor, political intrigue, and the pursuit of orthodoxy at any cost. Emerging in the 12th century as a response to perceived heresy within the Catholic Church, the Inquisition wielded its authority across Europe, leaving an indelible mark on the collective memory of the time.

The roots of the Inquisition can be traced back to the 11th century, when Pope Gregory VII and subsequent pontiffs sought to strengthen Church authority and combat perceived threats to doctrinal purity. The establishment of local tribunals, known as episcopal inquisitions, aimed to root out deviations from Catholic teachings, particularly among the Cathars and other dualist heresies prevalent in southern France and Italy.

However, it was not until the 13th century that the papacy formalized its approach with the creation of the Dominican Order-led Papal Inquisition. Founded by Pope Gregory IX in 1231, this institution marked a significant escalation in the Church's efforts to suppress dissent and enforce doctrinal conformity. The Dominicans, known for their rigorous adherence to orthodoxy and zealous pursuit of heretics, were tasked with investigating and prosecuting cases of heresy throughout Christendom.

The methods employed by the Inquisition were both systematic and severe. Inquisitors, appointed by the papacy and often granted sweeping powers, conducted inquiries (inquisitio) into suspected heretics, relying on interrogation, surveillance, and the testimonies of informants to build cases. The accused were subject to a range of punitive measures, from public penance and confiscation of property to imprisonment and, in extreme cases, execution by burning at the stake.

During the Middle Ages, the Catholic Church wielded tremendous power over religious and political affairs in Europe. As dissent grew against its authority, particularly from groups like the Waldenses, the Church responded with a systematic campaign of repression known as the Inquisition.

The Waldenses, adherents of a Christian movement that predated even the Protestant Reformation, found themselves in direct conflict with the Catholic Church due to their rejection of many Catholic doctrines and practices. Originating in the Alpine valleys of northern Italy and southeastern France, the Waldenses emphasized a return to the simplicity and purity of early Christianity, rejecting the wealth and hierarchy of the Catholic Church. They believed in the authority of Scripture and sought to live out their faith in accordance with what they understood from the Bible.

As the influence of the Waldenses spread, particularly during the 12th and 13th centuries, they faced increasing scrutiny and persecution from ecclesiastical authorities. The Catholic Church viewed them as heretics and a threat to its authority, launching numerous campaigns to suppress their movement. In response to the growing dissent and perceived threats to orthodoxy, Pope Lucius III in 1184 issued a decree declaring the suppression of heresy and the establishment of ecclesiastical tribunals to investigate and punish heretics—the birth of what became known as the medieval Inquisition.

The Inquisition was characterized by its ruthless methods of investigation and punishment. Heretics, including Waldenses, were subjected to torture, imprisonment, and execution if they refused to recant their beliefs. The Waldenses, known for their steadfast faith and refusal to renounce their principles, endured horrific persecution. They were hunted down in their mountain refuges, their homes burned, and many were massacred in efforts to eradicate their presence.

One of the most notorious episodes in Waldensian history was the Piedmontese Easter in 1655. In response to their persistent resistance and their refusal to conform to Catholic doctrines, the Duke of Savoy ordered a brutal campaign against the Waldenses in the Piedmont valleys. Thousands were massacred, including women and children, and their villages were pillaged and destroyed. Despite the atrocities, the Waldenses continued to endure, finding strength in their faith and in their communal bonds.

The Inquisition's ultimate decline came with the Age of Enlightenment and the rise of secular governance, which challenged its authority and methods. Yet, its imprint on European history remained profound, shaping perceptions of religious tolerance, judicial procedure, and the intersection of faith and power. The Inquisition serves as a cautionary tale of the dangers of unchecked authority and ideological conformity, a reminder that the quest for religious purity can exact a devastating toll on individual lives and societies as a whole.

APPENDIX 4
Historical Facts About the Waldenses

The history of the Waldenses is a remarkable story of a people who, despite centuries of persecution, remained steadfast in their faith and commitment to the teachings of the Bible. Their origins can be traced back to the early days of Christianity, particularly during the reign of Emperor Nero in Rome, when many Christians fled persecution and sought refuge in the rugged terrain of the Cottian Alps in northern Italy and southeastern France.

These remote and inaccessible valleys, known as the Piedmont Valleys, provided a natural sanctuary for the Waldenses, allowing them to preserve their distinct beliefs and practices. The steep cliffs, narrow passes, and dense forests of the Alps formed a formidable barrier against their persecutors, enabling the Waldenses to maintain their way of life for centuries.

The Waldenses, also referred to as the Vaudois or the People of the Valleys, considered themselves the direct descendants of the apostolic church. They adhered to a simple, Bible-based faith that emphasized humility and a deep reverence for the Scriptures. Unlike the Roman Catholic Church, which they believed had deviated from the true teachings of Christ, the Waldenses sought to live according to the principles laid out in the New Testament.

One of the defining characteristics of the Waldenses was their commitment to making the Bible accessible to all. They were among the first to translate the Scriptures into their native language, known as the Romaunt language. This emphasis on vernacular translations allowed the common people to read and interpret the Bible for themselves, a practice that was highly controversial in an era when the Catholic Church closely guarded access to religious texts.

From their secluded valleys, the Waldenses sent out missionaries to share their faith throughout Europe. These missionaries, known as the Barbes, traveled in pairs and often disguised themselves as merchants or craftsmen to avoid detection. They carried with them portions of the Scriptures and religious tracts, which they discretely shared with those they encountered on their journeys.

Despite their peaceful nature and commitment to a simple, Christ-like life, the Waldenses faced relentless persecution from the Catholic Church and the Inquisition. Accused of heresy, they endured numerous campaigns of violence and oppression designed to eradicate their presence. The most notorious of these was the Piedmontese Easter Massacre of 1655, during which thousands of Waldenses were brutally slaughtered.

Yet, in the face of such unimaginable cruelty, the Waldenses remained resolute in their faith. Their unwavering devotion to God and their willingness to sacrifice everything for their beliefs became a symbol of religious freedom and resistance against tyranny. The Waldensian story inspired admiration and support from Protestant reformers across Europe, who saw in their struggle a reflection of their own efforts to break free from the control of the Catholic Church.

Over the centuries, the Waldenses' history of perseverance and faithfulness has continued to inspire people around the world. Notable figures, such as Ellen G. White, a prominent American Christian author, visited the Waldensian valleys and documented their story, ensuring that their legacy would be preserved for future generations.

GLOSSARY
Important Terms and Their Meanings

Acrid: Having a sharp, bitter smell or taste.

Acts of the Apostles: A book in the New Testament of the Bible, detailing the early history of the Christian church.

Alcove: A small recessed section of a room or wall.

Ambrose: An influential 4th-century Christian bishop of Milan.

Ambush: A surprise attack by people lying in wait in a concealed position.

Anvils: Heavy iron blocks used in forging and shaping metal.

Apprehension: A feeling of anxiety or fear about the future; the act of arresting or seizing someone.

Archangel: A high-ranking angel mentioned in various parts of the Bible.

Archbishop: A senior bishop who oversees a large ecclesiastical jurisdiction.

Assailant: A person who physically attacks another.

Augustine: A prominent 4th-5th century Christian theologian and philosopher.

Avignon: A city in southeastern France, historically significant as the seat of the papacy in the 14th century.

Baptism: A Christian sacrament of admission and adoption, almost invariably with the use of water.

Beatific: Showing or feeling great happiness or serenity.

Black Death: A devastating pandemic of bubonic plague that struck Europe in the mid-14th century.

Blasphemer: A person who speaks irreverently about God or sacred things.

Bolt (of cloth): A rolled length of fabric, typically of a standard size.

Breach: A gap in a wall, barrier, or defense.

Bucklers: Small, round shields used for protection in hand-to-hand combat.

Cacophony: A harsh, discordant mixture of sounds; a din.

Callused: Having areas of thick, hardened skin due to repeated friction or pressure.

Cathedrals: The principal church of a diocese, containing the bishop's throne.

Cloak: A sleeveless outer garment, typically a long cape.

Cobblestones: A natural stone, typically rounded, used to pave streets.

Copyist (or Scribe): A person who makes written copies of documents or manuscripts.

Corruption: Dishonest or fraudulent conduct by those in power.

Cottian Alps: A mountain range in the southwestern part of the Alps, along the French-Italian border.

Cowl: A large loose hood, particularly one worn by a monk.

Croissants: Crescent-shaped, flaky pastries of Austrian origin, popular in France.

Crusade: A medieval military expedition, typically called by the Pope, to recover the Holy Land from Muslim rule. In this context, it refers to the campaign against the Waldensians.

Cudgel: A short, thick stick used as a weapon.

Curdling: The process of coagulating milk to form curds, which are used to make cheese.

Cured meats: Meats preserved through processes like salting, drying, or smoking.

Damascus: An ancient city mentioned in the Bible, now the capital of Syria.

Dappled: Marked with spots or patches of different shades or colors.

Defiance: The act of openly resisting or challenging authority in defense of one's beliefs or values.

Denier: A small French coin of little value. The livre was divided into twenty sous. Each sous was made up of twelve deniers.

Deus vult: Latin phrase meaning "God wills it," used as a battle cry by crusaders.

Din: A loud, unpleasant, and prolonged noise.

Diocese: A district under the pastoral care of a bishop in Catholic churches.

Dismayed: Feeling distressed or discouraged in the face of trouble or disappointment.

Dogma: A principle or set of principles laid down by an authority as incontrovertibly true.

Drawled: Spoke in a slow, lazy way.

Eerie: Strange and frightening.

Embers: The glowing remnants of a fire, mentioned in the chapter during the characters' struggle to keep the wolves at bay.

Embroidery: Decorative needlework on cloth.

Envoy: A representative or messenger, especially one on a diplomatic mission.

Exhilaration: A feeling of excitement, happiness, or elation.

Fanaticism: Excessive enthusiasm or zeal, especially in religious matters.

Fetid: Having a strong, offensive smell.

Filament: A very fine thread or wire.

Flagellants: Religious zealots who publicly whipped themselves as a form of penance and to ward off divine punishment.

Gilded: Covered thinly with gold leaf or gold paint.

Gnarled: Knobbly, rough, and twisted, especially referring to tree branches or, in this case, a walking stick. Weather-beaten in appearance.

Gorge: A narrow valley between hills or mountains, typically with steep rocky walls and a stream running through it.

Grenoble: A city in southeastern France, at the foot of the French Alps.

Hawkers: People who travel about selling goods, typically advertising them by shouting.

Heady: Having a strong or exhilarating effect.

Heirloom: A valuable object that has belonged to a family for several generations.

Henchman: A faithful follower or supporter, especially one prepared to engage in crime or violence.

Heresy: Belief or opinion contrary to orthodox religious doctrine.

Heretic: A person believing in or practicing religious heresy.

Holy Father: A title used to refer to the Pope in the Roman Catholic Church.

Hypocrisy: The practice of claiming to have moral standards or beliefs to which one's own behavior does not conform.

Illuminated, The: The name of the secret group of Waldensian believers that Lucien joins.

Illuminated: (In the context of manuscripts) Decorated with gold, silver, or brilliant colors.

Incontrovertibly: In a way that is not able to be denied or disputed.

Indulgences: In Catholic theology, a way to reduce the amount of punishment one has to undergo for sins.

Inheritance: In the biblical context, this term refers to the eternal reward promised by God to those who serve Him faithfully.

Inquisition: A powerful institution within the Catholic Church that was responsible for identifying, investigating, and punishing individuals accused of heresy or deviating from Church doctrine.

Inquisitor: An official in the Inquisition responsible for investigating and prosecuting heresy.

Iron maiden: A purported medieval torture device, consisting of an iron cabinet with a hinged front and spike-covered interior, sufficiently tall to enclose a human being.

Jerkin: A close-fitting jacket, often made of leather.

Kindred Spirits: People who share the same beliefs, attitudes, or feelings.

Kneading: The process of working dough with the hands to develop gluten, used in baking bread.

Labyrinth: A complicated irregular network of passages or paths.

Linen: A strong cloth made from flax fibers.

Lux Lucet in Tenebris: Latin phrase meaning "Light shines in the darkness," used as a password.

Lyon: Formerly spelled in English as Lyons, is a city in east-central France where much of the action in chapter 23 takes place.

Maelstrom: A powerful whirlpool in the sea; figuratively, a state of confused movement or violent turmoil.

Manuscripts: Books or documents, often ancient and significant, written by hand rather than typed or printed.

Martyred: Killed because of one's beliefs, especially religious beliefs.

Martyrs: People who suffer death for their religious or other beliefs.

Menace: A person or thing that is likely to cause harm; a threat or danger.

Miasma: An unpleasant or unhealthy smell or vapor.

Nondescript: Lacking distinctive or interesting features or characteristics.

Orchard: A piece of land planted with fruit trees. The farmhouse has an orchard of apple and pear trees.

Ordeal: A severe trial or experience, representative of the characters' struggle and flight from persecution.

Outpost: A small military camp or position at some distance from the main army, used to watch for the enemy.

Pallet: A straw-filled mattress or hard bed.

Parchment: A writing material made from the prepared skin of an animal.

Pastries: Sweet baked goods made with dough.

Pawn: To deposit an object as security for money borrowed.

Persecution: Hostile and oppressive treatment, especially because of religious beliefs. The characters seek refuge from persecution.

Pestilence: A fatal epidemic disease, particularly bubonic plague.

Pike: A long thrusting spear used by infantry.

Piqued: Stimulated or aroused, especially in regards to interest or curiosity. feeling of unease or apprehension.

Plague hospitals: Makeshift medical facilities set up to treat victims of the Black Death.

Pragelas: A valley in the Cottian Alps, historically significant for Waldensian settlements.

Prickled: A sensation similar to being pricked by something sharp, often used to describe a

Providence: The protective care of God or of nature as a spiritual power.

Provisions: Supplies of food and other necessities.

Purgatory: In Catholic doctrine, a place or state of suffering inhabited by the souls of sinners who are expiating their sins before going to heaven.

Pyres: Large fires used to burn the bodies of plague victims to prevent further spread of the disease.

Quiche: A savory tart consisting of pastry crust filled with eggs, milk, cheese, and other ingredients.

Quill: A writing instrument made from a feather.

Rack: An instrument of torture consisting of a frame on which the victim was stretched by turning rollers to which the wrists and ankles were tied.

Recognition: The act of identifying or acknowledging someone or something as familiar.

Refuge: Similar to sanctuary, a place offering protection or shelter, especially for those fleeing danger or persecution.

Relics: Objects of religious veneration, especially a part of a deceased holy person's body or belongings.

Rendezvous point: A pre-arranged meeting place.

Repercussions: Unintended consequences or effects, often negative, that result from an action or decision.

Reproved: Expressed disapproval or criticism of someone.

Resurrection: The concept of rising from the dead, central to Christian belief.

Reviled: Criticized in an abusive or hostile way.

Righteousness: The quality of being morally right or justifiable.

Rubies: Precious gemstones, used metaphorically in the chapter to emphasize the value of the scriptures.

Rugged: Having a rough, uneven surface. Describes the snow-capped peaks surrounding the valley.

Rye: A type of grain used to make bread.

Sacraments: Religious ceremonies or acts of the Catholic Church.

Sage: In this context, the title given to the wise leader of the Illuminated.

Sanctuary: A place of refuge or safety.

Satchel: A bag carried on the shoulder, typically used for carrying books.

Saul (Paul): A key figure in early Christianity, known for his dramatic conversion on the road to Damascus.

Scavenged: Searched for and collected from discarded materials.

Scribbling: The act of writing or making notes in a hurried or informal manner.

Scribe (or Copyist): A person who copies out documents, especially a person employed to do this before printing was invented.

Scriptorium: A room in medieval European monasteries devoted to the copying, writing, or illuminating of manuscripts by monastic scribes.

Scriptures: The sacred writings of Christianity contained in the Bible.

Sect: A religious or political group that has separated from a larger organization due to differences in beliefs.

Shale: Soft, finely stratified sedimentary rock that splits easily into thin layers.

Shawl: A piece of fabric worn by women over the shoulders or head.

Shingles: Thin, flat pieces of wood used as a roof covering. The farmhouse has a roof made of weathered wood shingles.

Shroud: cover or envelop so as to conceal from view.

Snick: A sharp clicking sound, often associated with a latch or lock.

Sola scriptura: Latin phrase meaning "by scripture alone," a theological doctrine that the Bible is the sole source of authority for Christian faith and practice.

Sous: A former French coin of low value. The livre was divided into twenty sous. Each sous was made up of twelve deniers.

Spectacles: An old term for eyeglasses. The first spectacles were made in central Italy by about 1290.

Steadfast: Resolutely or dutifully firm and unwavering.

Strappado: A form of torture where the victim's hands are tied behind their back and suspended by a rope attached to their wrists.

Subterfuge: Deceit used in order to achieve one's goal.

Suspicion: A feeling of mistrust or doubt about someone or something.

Sylvester: Refers to Pope Sylvester I, who was Pope from 314 to 335 AD.

Throng: A large, densely packed crowd of people.

Tome: A book, especially a large, heavy, scholarly one.

Town crier: A person who makes public announcements in the streets or marketplace of a town.

Transcription: The act of making a written copy of something. The characters transcribe ancient manuscripts.

Trepidation: A feeling of fear or anxiety about something that may happen.

Tribunal: A court of justice.

Triumph: A feeling of great satisfaction or achievement.

Tunic: A simple slip-on garment made with or without sleeves and usually knee-length or longer.

Turin: A city in northern Italy, near where many Waldensians settled.

Unquenchable: Unable to be quenched or satisfied.

Valais: A region in southern Switzerland.

Valdese: Another term for Waldensian, referring to the Christian movement.

Vaulted: Having an arched roof or ceiling.

Waldensians or Waldenses: A religious sect that was considered heretical by the dominant Church authority during the Middle Ages. They emphasized a life of simplicity, freedom, and adherence to the teachings of the Bible.

Wan: Pale; tired and unhealthy in appearance.

Wares: Goods or merchandise, especially those offered for sale.

Weathered: Worn by exposure to the elements, especially over time.

Wizened: Shriveled or wrinkled with age.

Wrath: Extreme anger, often associated with a desire for punishment or vengeance.

Yew: A type of evergreen tree, often used for making bows due to its strong, flexible wood.

Zealous: Having or showing fervor for a cause, often to a fanatical degree, describing Inquisitor Talbot's attitude toward rooting out heresy.

www.ingramcontent.com/pod-product-compliance
Lightning Source LLC
Chambersburg PA
CBHW071323140726
47996CB00005B/1800